WISHING
STEPS

Danna Walters

NewLink Publishing
Henderson, Nevada
2019

WISHING STEPS
Danna Walters

This book is a work of pure fiction composed from the author's imagination. It is protected under the copyright laws of the United States of America. No part of this publication may be reproduced or transmitted in any form or by any means, electronic or mechanical, including photocopying, recording, or by an information storage or retrieval system, without written permission from the publisher. Contact the publisher at info@ newlinkpublishing.com.

Line/Content Editor: Janelle Evans
Interior Design: Donna Raymon
Cover: Richard R. Draude

p. cm. — Danna Walters (Paranormal fiction/time travel.
Copyright © 2019 / Danna Walters
All Rights Reserved

ISBN: 978-1-948266-03-1/Paperback
ISBN: 978-1-948266-36-6/E-Pub

1. Fiction/Romance/Time Travel.
2. Fiction/Romance/Historical
3. Fiction/Romance/General

www.newlinkpublishing.com
Henderson, NV 89002
Printed in the United States of America

12345678910

DEDICATION

I'd like to express my heartfelt thanks to Jo, Richard, Denice and Janelle at New Link Publishing for their help and support in bringing my book to readers and making me a better writer.

Thanks, also to friends who travel with us down paths that nourish my imagination and allow it to soar. Tom & Jessica, Tammy & Rob, Ken & Melanie, Ric & Eddie, Mike & Rita, Dave & Jan, Margie and Sherry.

CHAPTER 1
Many Moons Away

Running across the ancient Druid's Circle, mist swirled around my ankles. I searched for Erin, my five-year-old daughter. In the center of the Druid's grounds, I called out for her into the darkness.

"Over here, Momma. I'm making a wish!" Her voice floated up from the nearby Wishing Steps. Clouds moved away from the full moon, lighting the way.

"Erin, no. Don't!" Running toward the steps, the damp ferns brushed against my legs. I couldn't reach her soon enough.

"I did it, Momma! I did it! I walked backward all the way up the steps with my eyes closed, all by myself. Now the Druid King must grant my wish!"

My heart weighed heavy in my chest, seeing her standing at the top of the step, beaming in the silver light of the moon. The dread washing over me left a fine sheen of sweat on my skin.

Waking with moist eyes, I lay still, trying to decipher the dream. My husband, Cian, and I had taken Erin to Ireland for her fifth birthday to see his and my families' homeland. She, of course, excited about seeing a real castle, wore her tiara and princess gown everywhere we went in Ireland. We stayed at the Blarney Castle Hotel, where she made a wish on the Wishing Step. It didn't bother me then, so the dream perplexed me.

Unable to shake the worry caused by the troubling dream, my body jolted at the burst of wind that banged the shutter on my bedroom's open window.

Cian continued to snore beside me. I envy the man's uncanny ability to sleep like the dead.

Throwing back the covers and swinging my legs off the side of the bed, I stepped across the cool, wood floor to secure the shutter. Peering out the window, the cliff edge drew my gaze. I couldn't see much except the wind buffeting the royal palms that ruled the view to the cliff and ocean beyond.

Dark clouds moved across the moon, obscuring the trees. Goose pimples chased over my skin. I ran back to bed, my white cotton nightgown billowing at my back. Sliding under the covers, I snuggled close to Cian's warm, sleeping form. I tried hard to blot out the thought of the young, distraught Irish wife, Mira, who threw herself off the cliff. Sent to the island as slaves in the 1600's, she no longer wanted to live after losing her husband.

Instead, I concentrated on my own husband's snoring until I drifted to sleep to the sound of rain beating on our tin roof.

The smell of bacon permeated my senses. Yawning, I sat up, running a hand over the empty sheets beside me. A smile flitted across my face. Cian must be the cause of the wonderful aromas wafting up the stairs.

Our five-year-old baby girl flew into the room and jumped onto the bed, her exuberance each morning infectious—usually.

"Momma! I have to go check on Iris. Palm branches are lying everywhere outside! I bet Iris is scared." She continued to bounce on her knees. "Please Momma? Please? I'll come back for breakfast as soon as I see she's okay." Erin held her clasped hands under her chin, waiting for my answer.

"Okay, okay. Stop with the bouncing already. Go get your rain boots on, and I'll get my robe. We'll see that your pony's fine, give her some breakfast, and then come back in for ours." I rubbed the sleep from my eyes.

"Yippee!" Erin leapt off the bed and raced from the room.

Falling back into my pillow with my arms spread out beside me, I contemplated coffee.

Erin bounded back into the room sporting her purple rain boots with her pajamas. "Momma, let's go!" She tugged on my hand.

"I'm coming." I threw off the covers and got out of bed, picking up a light blue silk robe laying across my mother's chair. The chair I'd placed in front of the French doors leading to our balcony.

My little girl darted into the closet and reemerged with my black rain boots with daisies on them. The two of us clomped down the stairs into the kitchen.

"All elephants must eat outside," Cian said flipping pancakes at the stove with his back to us.

"Da, we're not elephants. It's me and momma." Erin put her hands on her hips.

"Oh, aye. Ye sounded like a herd of elephants coming down the stairs." Cian turned and winked at me.

Sliding my arms around his waist, I laid my head against his back. Beneath my cheek his muscles rippled with the next pancake he flipped in the air.

"I just can't resist you in your blue, plaid pajama bottoms," I said.

"Sure me standing in the kitchen cooking breakfast has nothing to do with it?" He looked over his shoulder at me.

"I must admit it adds to the appeal." I grinned.

"Mommy, come on. We have to go see Iris!" Erin tugged at my hand.

Cian quirked an eyebrow at me.

Okay, so I tended to give in to her every whim, how could I deny that cherubic face? "We are going to ease Erin's fear and see to it that Iris made it through the storm just fine. We'll be right back for breakfast."

"Aye, now I see the need for rain boots." Leaning down, he scooped Erin up into his arms and carried our squealing child out to the porch. I followed, not able to help the big grin spreading across my face. He locked eyes with Erin and spoke in a serious tone to her. "Your granddad, Emilio, and I built that barn. No wind, not even Antigua's trade winds are going to blow it down." He put her down on the steps and tousled her hair. "Now, go tell your pony what I said so she knows not to be afraid. Be quick or I'll eat your share of bacon."

Following Erin out to the barn, I smiled at her high spirits and marveled at her small footprints even in rain boots. Good thing we wore them. The tropical storm left the path to the barn a treacherous, muddy mess.

I entered to find her arms wrapped around Iris' neck, murmuring assurances in her pony's ear.

"All right little miss, Iris is fine. Come get a scoop or two of these oats for her." I lifted the top off the barrel that stored oats. On her tippy toes she could barely reach down far enough in the barrel to scoop the oats, but she insisted on doing it herself. Her fierce, independent spirit made Cian proud.

"Okay momma, we'd better go eat our breakfast now, before Daddy eats my bacon!" She turned and ran out of the barn, leaving me holding the lid.

The sun streaming through the sliding glass door bathed our wee Erin in light, setting her strawberry blonde hair to an imaginary flame. My tears threatened to make an appearance, listening and watching her and Cian laugh and tease each other while we ate the pancakes Cian made.

Just six years earlier, I buried my last known relative, Granddad Irish. Feeling forlorn and abandoned, my hollow life changed at the discovery of an old trunk with a letter from Granddad Irish. The letter brought back childhood memories and led me on a journey to Ireland and Antigua, where I reconnected with Cian. Now here I sat across the table from the man of my dreams and our sweet daughter—my own dear family. A reality too good to be true.

"Irelyn, love, come back to us. Ye look like ye were many moons away." Cian's expressive gaze asked me if I were okay. Since having Erin, we had learned how to communicate in various ways in order to avoid waking or troubling her.

"Da, she's right here eating pancakes. Isn't there only one moon?" Erin dipped another bite in a puddle of syrup.

Blinking my eyes and smiling at Cian, I said to Erin, "Yes, we have only one moon. One great big moon the entire world sees. It tells us when to go to bed, and it commands the tides of the oceans."

"Among other things," Cian said, muttering under his breath.

I cast a warning look his direction. Erin didn't know her da came from the past underneath a Blue Moon. I wanted to keep it that way, but how to explain the phrase, "many moons"? The sound of someone on the porch steps saved me from having to answer, at least, for now.

"Knock, knock, anyone home?" said Rosa. She and Emilio, Erin's adoptive grandparents, slid the door open and stepped into the kitchen.

"Nanny and Grampy!" Jumping out of her chair, Erin threw herself into Emilio's waiting arms.

"There's my little sunshine." Rosa leaned over and placed a kiss on Erin's forehead.

"What brings the two of you over on a Saturday morning? Not that ye aren't a welcome sight, ye understand."

"Well, Boss, I thought I'd see if the storm did any damage to the animal's houses." Emilio set Erin down and with a nudge said, "Finish your breakfast, little one."

"Here, help yourselves to some coffee and join us." I gestured to the coffee pot, though Rosa was well acquainted with my kitchen. She and Emilio lived in this house with Cian before the two of us married. A place she cooked and cleaned while Emilio helped Cian with the animals and land. Emilio still worked with Cian, and Rosa came over whenever I needed an extra hand, or just a break. They moved into the bungalow granddad Irish left me in his will. A wonderful arrangement that benefited all of us.

"Grampy, Da said no wind could blow down a building you and he put up."

"Is that so? Well, I reckon it would take a mighty big wind, bigger than we've experienced." With a wink in our direction, he said, "Cian, let's go check it out and clean up the palm fronds."

"No rest for the weary." Cian kissed me on the head. "Um, I cooked. You clean."

"Hey, if it means waking up to the aroma of coffee, pancakes and bacon…you bet." Grinning, I cleared off the table.

Cian and Emilio went outside with Erin in tow. Rosa helped herself to a cup of coffee. My heart filled with joy for our little family, but the feeling of dread from the dream lingered over me like a dark cloud.

CHAPTER 2
Sinking Stones

Looking out the window over the kitchen sink, I noticed Emilio squint his eyes against the bright sun. I watched Cian hand him a nail to hammer into the loose board on the side of the barn. The joy of watching those two men work together made me pause in rinsing the dishes. What were those two discussing? They appeared to be in a deep conversation.

"Rosa, I see Emilio left his hat on the counter. I'm going to run it out to him. The sun looks brutal today." Rosa started to get up. I motioned for her to stay seated. "Stay and enjoy your coffee. I'll just be a second."

"Fine by me." Rosa settled back down and raised her cup to me before taking a sip.

Crossing the yard with Emilio's hat in hand, I waved at the men. "Thought you might need this, Emilio." I placed the hat on top of his head.

"Gracias." Emilio adjusted his hat, smiling at me. "Your ears must've been burning. Just telling Cian it's high time he took you to Glass Water Cave."

"Wee Erin is still too young for the trek and climb. Guess we'll wait 'til she can make it."

"Why don't you let Rosa and me take her to the cove for a picnic today and you and Irelyn can have the day to yourselves. Show Irelyn the cave. She's been on the island too long not to have seen it."

Cian looked to me with his eyebrows raised. The thought of a full day alone with my handsome husband, sounded heavenly. Nodding, I couldn't suppress a grin.

"Well, if ye insist. Some time alone with me wife sounds too good to pass up." Cian clapped him on the back, grabbed me by the hand and we sprinted toward the house.

"Da!" Erin said the moment we came through the door. "Are we going for a ride now? Does Iris have her saddle on?"

"We'll not be going for a ride today, lass. Your Grampy said he and Nanny would take ye on a picnic to the cove today." Cian winked at me, his eyes lit with merriment.

I smiled seeing Erin slide out of her chair and throw her arms around Rosa. After a tight squeeze, she ran up the stairs as fast as her rain boots allowed. "I'll get my swimsuit on!" she said from above.

Laughing, Rosa took her cup to the sink. "I guess my day has been planned for me, and I couldn't have planned it better. From the glint in Cian's eye, I'd say he has a plan of his own."

"Actually, the plan came from your kind, thoughtful husband. Cian is just smart enough to follow through with it."

"Ye will need to wear your swimsuit as well as your hiking boots. I'm going to show ye a special place on the island called Glass Water Cave." Taking me by the hand, he led me toward the stairs.

"Ahhh, that's a special place. Time you saw it, certainly. You kids have fun!"

"Thank you, Rosa. You have my cell number if you need me. Have fun," I said over my shoulder before ascending the stairs to get dressed.

Erin didn't often go anywhere without either Cian or I, but there lived no one I trusted more than her honorary grandparents, Emilio and Rosa. She would be fine with the two of them watching her. It helped me shake off the unease that settled over me during the storm. I proceeded to get dressed for the day with Cian.

"How much further?" I called out to the back of Cian's head, his bicycle in front of mine. His shoulder blades glistened with sweat, and a wet streak showed through his tank top down his spine. Gripping the handlebars with one hand, I wiped the perspiration off my forehead with my other hand without slowing down.

"Not much...on bike." He hollered back over his shoulder. "This is where we leave the road. Careful of holes. Follow my path."

Staying close, I turned my bike off the road onto a narrow grassy path that left me no choice but to follow his lead.

The softer ground made the going slower, and the pedaling tougher. Lifting my head to call out to him for a break, my tense muscles relaxed at seeing him standing by his bicycle in a clearing. I pulled up next to him and slid from the seat, straddling my bike. Facing the coast, I took in the amazing view from this high advantage point.

"Oh, Cian, it's lovely! The island looks so lush and green from up here."

"That it is, but this isn't what I brought ye to see. We will walk our bikes from here. Too steep to ride, not to mention the drop off." He walked his bike toward a gravel path leading around a rock peak.

"Not to mention what? Did you say drop off?" My hands tightened on the handlebars. He didn't stop so I had no choice but to take a deep breath and follow after him.

The gravel path wound around the hill in a downward spiral. Drop off indeed. I walked as close as I could to the rock face with my bike separating me from the ridge.

The sun sparkled across the ocean below, making me long to be in the cooling water. Raising my face to fully enjoy the breeze, my feet slid out from under me. I let go of the bike to reach back for the rough ground rising fast to greet me. I had little time to inspect the damage to the heels of my hands before I realized my bike careened toward Cian.

"Watch out!" I called too late.

The errant bike crashed into Cian's bike, knocking it out of his hands to land in a heap with mine. Waving his arms out to his side like a goose about to take flight, he landed on top of the bikes. I laughed so hard tears ran down my face.

"Now what is it about me lying on top of this wreckage do ye find so amusing?" Cian brushed gravel and dust off his legs while getting his feet back under him. "Perchance it's the fact I could've rolled down the cliff side to me death? Hmm?"

"Oh, no, it's not that." I took a deep breath to calm my laughter. "It was the waving your arms around like a preening goose that did it." Laughter bubbled up inside me again. I couldn't control it.

"I think we better leave the bikes here while we trek the rest of the way." Shaking his head, he extended a hand to help me off the ground. He raised my hands to his lips, placing a gentle kiss on each, and I sobered right up.

After five minutes more of walking, Cian stopped without warning, tugging my hand to stop me from passing him. "This is it, Irelyn."

I didn't see anything we hadn't already seen. I shrugged my shoulders. "I don't see a cave."

"Look down there to your left." He pointed to what appeared to be a hole in the ground at the base of the rock face. "We climb down into the cave."

Placing my hands on his broad shoulders, I peered around him to see what he expected of me. I liked adventure, but I leaned toward caution.

The entrance didn't require much climbing, really just a hop down. Cian jumped down first, then turned to help me.

Once inside the cave, I stood on a rock ledge looking into a small pool of water, clear as glass. It looked so inviting I couldn't wait to immerse myself. I stepped out of my shorts and peeled off my tank top. I laid my clothes on a rock, safe from splashing, and adjusted the straps to my bathing suit.

"Let's jump!" Cian stripped off his tank top and dropped it at his feet.

"Wait!" I held onto his arm, keeping him on the ledge. "It's too shallow. Be careful."

Laughing, he pushed me off the ledge and jumped in after me. I expected my feet to touch bottom without my hair getting wet. My eyes widened when I plunged all the way under. The water, deep enough to put my treading skills to work. "Wow! It looks about three feet deep."

"I know, it's because it's so clear." He slung the hair back out of his face, showering me with sprinkles. "I'd say it's about six feet deep. See the wee creatures swimming around?"

"Oh, what are they?" I moved closer to Cian, prepared to hop on his back if need be. Many see-through creatures, about half an inch long, swam in the water with us.

"They're fresh water shrimp. I think."

"Look up there, Cian! See how this rock doesn't go all the way up to the ceiling?"

"What do ye say we climb up and see what's on the other side?" He lifted himself out of the water with ease and turned to help me out. I braced my feet on the rocks lining the fresh water pool, using his pulling hand to give me the leverage to climb out. Sufficiently cooled off, I didn't mind leaving the water to the shrimp like creatures.

I laid on my stomach next to Cian at the top of the rock, near the ceiling. Sure enough, the cavern had another side. I gathered a few rocks and handed some to Cian. We dropped them into the darkness. The small rocks made a soft splash. The other side contained water as well. "Scary. Anything could be in that water." I shivered thinking about the unknown on the dark side of the cave. Things, like people, are not always what they appear to be.

"Well, it's like the future, is it not? Like we dropped our stones into the darkness. We lay out our plans for the future, but for all our planning, we don't know what tomorrow holds." He laid a hand on my arm. "You're shivering, Irelyn. What do ye say we head back up now?"

"Yes, let's. Who knew I married such a philosopher?"

Chuckling, he helped me down from the rock. Before climbing out of the cave he drew me into his arms. "Irelyn, I love ye today more than I loved ye the day we wed. Whatever our future holds, we'll experience it together, now won't we, a ghra?" He touched his forehead to mine. Five plus years of marriage and I still go soft when he calls me "love" in Irish.

"There's no one, Cian Gallagher, I'd rather face uncertainty with." I grinned at him.

Bathed in a circle of sunlight, he tightened his hold on me and crushed my lips to his. Tilting my head back, I deepened the kiss. My hands slid to his hips, pulling him even closer.

He broke away on a groan. "We best be going before I slip that swim suit off ye." Turning to climb up, he put his hand on the rock entrance.

"Cian, what's that under your hand? It looks like a carving of some sort." His hand lifted away, giving me an even better look.

"Someone carved their initials," he said. "E.W. loves W.K."

"How sweet. Now, let's get in the sunshine."

"Hey, W.K. is Wendy Kincaid's initials. Do ye think it could be hers? Nah, how would she have gotten down here?"

11

"Right. There are probably many people with the same initials, especially after all this time."

He made quick work of climbing up the grass covered, rocky incline. At the top he squatted to give me a hand out of the cave. Standing in the sunshine, I rubbed the chill off my arms. Cian, always a gentleman, propelled both of our bikes all the way back up to the road.

M eanwhile at Shell Cove…

Rosa left Emilio and Erin playing in the sea. The three of them had been swimming for a good hour. Her stomach grumbled. Leaning over, she grabbed a beach towel off the sheet and dried her face and arms before reaching for the picnic basket and cooler. She set to work laying out turkey sandwiches, strawberry slices, and chips on paper plates for the three of them.

"Emilio! You and Erin, come out of the water now to eat some lunch!" The sun shone high in the sky, and the gentle waves didn't break until they reached shore. But even with perfect swimming conditions, the little one needed a break.

"Okay, Nanny!" Erin took long steps out of the water, jumping over the white foam on shore. "Can we build a sandcastle after I eat?" She plopped down on a corner of the sheet. Water dripped from her hair and chin onto the plate Rosa handed her.

"I'm starving! I could eat a whole sea monster," Emilio said joining the girls on the sheet.

Shaking her head and frowning in mock disapproval, Rosa said to Erin, "Can you believe how silly your grampy is?" Erin covered her mouth, full with a bite of sandwich, and giggled.

Rosa smiled, acknowledging Erin's good manners. "Oh! Look at the butterfly! It looks like it's standing on the rock. I've never seen one land on the tip of its wings before." Rosa shielded her eyes and pointed across the beach to the large rock.

"Is it blue? I see a blue one all the time. I think it likes to follow me around." Erin shrugged her shoulders and took another bite of her sandwich without glancing at the butterfly.

She thought a butterfly followed her around? What an endearing thing to believe. Rosa shared a smile with Emilio over Erin's head.

"Come on, Grampy. Let's build a sandcastle." Erin swung around to face the beach, her little hands pushing and gathering the warm sand into a mound.

"Hmm, are we going to build a castle or bury you up to your scrawny neck?" Emilio sat on the other side of her sand mound.

"Castle! Like the one in Ireland." Twisting around, she looked at Rosa. "Is my neck scrawny?"

"Your neck is absolutely perfect. Don't listen to your grampy. When your castle is finished we need to head back home."

Rosa closed the cooler and stood to shake sand out of the towels before stuffing them in the beach bag. She looked around to see what else needed packing. Not seeing anything else, she stood smiling at the banter Erin and Emilio exchanged over their sandcastle building efforts.

With one last look back on the days fun, Rosa watched the incoming tide wash away the sandcastle. Just like everything else in life—nothing last forever. She squelched a sigh and caught up with Emilio and Erin. Taking Erin's other hand, she walked toward the trail leading out of the cove, helping Emilio swing Erin between them.

CHAPTER 3
News From Ireland

"Irelyn, ye have a phone call from Cork!" Cian stood on the porch overlooking the garden. I had to shield the sun from my eyes to see him waving my phone above his head.

Hmm. I wonder what that's about. "I'll be right there!" I wiped my hands on my gardening apron and carried the basket of strawberries to the porch.

Erin and Cian liked the fruit in their oatmeal, cereal, toast, and their pancakes. They especially liked them on Rosa's cheesecakes, or by themselves in a big bowl—pretty much however they could get them. They loved their strawberries.

Handing Cian the basket, I took the phone and sat in one of the Adirondack chairs on the porch. "Hello?"

"Irelyn, be that you?"

I recognized my third cousin's voice right away. I first met Colleen as the front desk help for the hotel in Ireland where I stayed before I came to Antigua. It wasn't until later that I found out we were related.

Her grandmother by the same name was my granddad Irish's youngest sibling. Although I didn't get to meet her mother, Jewell, or the elder Colleen until we took Erin for her fifth birthday, I did get to meet my great uncle, Kyle. He and Colleen were the last living siblings of granddad Irish. Devastated by my granddad Irish's death, I appreciated meeting some of his family and being able to talk about him to others who knew and loved him.

"Yes, Colleen. I'm so happy to hear from you so soon after our trip. Erin still talks about her cousins that live close to a castle. We all had such a great time getting to know our relatives in Ireland." I couldn't tame the smile on my face.

"Irelyn, I'm glad to be talking to you, too. Be that as it may, Ma asked me to call. She would've called herself, except she's taking this really hard."

My hand gripped the phone at the unmistakable note of sadness in Colleen's voice. "What's wrong?" I whispered.

"It's Uncle Kyle. He passed in his sleep night before last. Ma wants you to know about the funeral arrangements."

"I'm so sorry, Colleen." Tears welled up in my eyes. I had to swallow the lump in my throat to continue. "I'll try to make it for the funeral. Give your ma a hug for me."

Before ringing off she gave me the funeral arrangements. I sat there fighting back tears with the phone in my lap.

Cian came back out on the porch from putting the strawberries up. "What is it, lass?" He set the phone aside and pulled me up to stand facing him.

Taking a deep breath, I told him about my great uncle Kyle's passing. "Do you think we can swing another trip to Ireland so soon? We were just there six months ago." I leaned my head on his shoulder.

"Of course we can. I just wish we could go by ship." His heavy sigh moved my head. I doubt he would ever get over his dislike of flying.

I offered him a half smile and said in my best Cian Irish brogue, "Whatever our future holds, we'll face it together, now won't we, a ghra?"

Shaking his head, but smiling nonetheless, he said, "Let's go book our flight. Erin will be pleased for sure." He led me into the house.

CHAPTER 4
Keeping Sheep

"Mommy, Daddy looks green." Erin patted Cian's face. He helped her out of the rental car.

"He'll be okay. Your Da doesn't like to fly, you know." Kissing Cian on the cheek, I took Erin by the hand and led her up to the front door of my great uncle Kyle's residence.

The house sat at the end of a country lane on thirty acres of grass as green as a Luna Caterpillar. Sheep being the family business, we drove past pastures dotted with the white tufted, fluffy animals. Erin had rolled down her window and waved to the animals, convinced she recognized several of them, and they her.

She could barely contain her excitement, stepping across the flag stones that led to the front door of the large, two story, stone house.

With two white paned windows resting on either side of the door, upstairs and down, the farmhouse looked more like a manor to me. "Cian, look at the wild rose growing on the front corner of the house. It's so lovely. Oh, the entry to the front door is covered in ivy. How could I have missed that when we came for Erin's birthday?" Not hearing a response, I turned to look at him. "You're going to be okay, aren't you?"

"I'm all right, but as long as I live, I'll never grow used to a large chunk of metal flying across the sky with yours truly in it." He raised a wary eye at a jet that flew over. Releasing a deep breath, he knocked on the door and took a step back, putting an arm around my shoulders. Erin filled the waiting silence by bouncing on her toes.

"Maybe they didn't hear you, Da. Let me knock." Stepping up to the door, Erin rapped as hard as she could below the black wreath hanging

17

there.

"That should raise the dead." Cian nodded at Erin.

"Really?" I said. How could he use that phrase? We were here because of the death of my great uncle Kyle.

"Sorry." Cian dropped his gaze, looking sheepish.

Leaning over, I gave him a peck on the cheek. "Let's walk around to see if there are any cars here. Doesn't sound as if anyone's home." Hand in hand, I walked with them around the corner.

Lace curtains hung in the windows on the side of the house. My internal wave of joy at the sight crashed, remembering the lace curtains of my mom's that I left hanging for many years after her passing. I don't suppose one ever gets over losing a loved one.

"Hello there!" A robust woman with graying hair swept up in a bun waved to us. Carrying an empty laundry basket on her hip, she ducked under a damp dish towel hanging on the line to come toward us.

"Good afternoon to ye. Might ye tell us where the owners of this house be?" Cian gave her his most persuasive grin.

Her wary look didn't change, so I said, "Colleen and her daughter, Jewell, are my great aunt and cousin. We've come from Antigua for my great uncle Kyle's funeral. Did you know him?"

"Oh sure! That I did. He and my grandfather were mates in school. I'm sorry, I heard of his passing. Colleen and my mother are the best of friends. If you wish to see Colleen or Jewel, you'll need to go to the hospital in Cork. That's where the ambulance took 'em." Having made that startling announcement, she turned toward the house with the basket.

For a moment I watched her walk away. Cian looked at me with his eyebrows raised. Erin, acting as oblivious as any child, picked a dandelion.

"Ma'am? Could you please tell us what happened?" I tucked my hair behind my ears in an effort to keep the wind from blowing it in my eyes. I should be used to tousled, windswept hair after living in Antigua with the constant trade winds, but having it in my eyes while talking to someone annoyed me even more.

"Don't rightly know," she said without turning around. "I'm just helping out. They carried Mrs. Colleen out on a stretcher. Jewell climbed in the back after her and off the ambulance tore. Ran right over the daisies. Colleen will be none too pleased about that, I tell you."

Swallowing the lump in my throat, I looked at Cian. "I guess we'd better get to the hospital."

He took me by the hand, leading me back to the car. "Come along, Erin." He called over his shoulder.

An elderly gentleman at the hospital information desk pointed us in the right direction. A flash of bright red hair coming toward us down the hallway caught my eye. The hair, as I suspected, belonged to my younger third cousin, Colleen.

"I'm so sorry we weren't home to greet you. It appears grandmother has suffered a stroke." Tears sprang to her eyes.

I offered her silent encouragement, laying my hand on her arm.

"Ma is with her now. I came straight over from the Inn. They'll only allow one in at a time until she's stable." Her voice cracked on the last word.

"Let's have a seat while we wait to speak with your ma." Cian led us to a group of chairs in a corner of the waiting room, a short walk from the information desk. Erin picked up a puzzle and turned the pieces out on the floor.

"Uncle Kyle will be laid to rest at the All Saints Cemetery in Blarney in only two days time. I'm sure Ma is more than a bit overwhelmed." I touched her arm when she swiped a tear off her cheek. I didn't know what to say to make her feel better. Jewel walked in looking much thinner than she did six months earlier. No doubt, caring for great uncle Kyle, her mother, and the farm, had taken its toll. My expectant gaze only brought a head shake from her.

"Ma had a massive stroke. They're keeping her sedated. Rest is the best thing for her. The Doctor doesn't know if she'll recover or how much she'll recover. They just don't know. They don't know anything! Why don't they know?" Her voice rose with each word. People lifted their heads to look our way.

"Here now, come, have a seat." Cian put an arm around her and guided her to a chair.

On the arm of her mother's chair, Colleen found a seat and held her hand.

Not knowing what to say, or how to comfort them made tears well

19

up in my eyes. I'd lost both of my parents to a car wreck while still fairly young. The helpless frustration I experienced, watching them both lay there dying in the hospital, had pressed like an enormous weight on my soul. I reached a hand out and laid it on top of Jewel and Colleen's.

"People recover every day from strokes. Her brain and body need time to rest and heal." Maybe she wouldn't, but offering them hope seemed like the right thing to do. I glanced at Cian. "We will stay here in Ireland to help out until she's able to go home. Try not to worry about anything, Jewel."

"Oh, blessings! It'd be such a gift if you could help with the sheep. Colleen has her own work up at the Inn. So kind of you, it is for sure." Tears spilled over her pale cheeks.

"For sure we will. Don't ye worry. I took care of a sheep or two as a young lad here in County Cork me self." He smirked and sent a wink my way, I being the only other one knowing the time he referred to was the 1600's.

Cian grew up in 1600's Ireland and Antigua. Under a blue moon, with the help of Ms. Caleah, an obeah, he came forward to my time.

"And Grand-dad Irish, your uncle Liam, told me quite a bit about keeping sheep. We will do fine. Erin will be thrilled!" Trying to look confident, I smiled at her.

"We best be going. It's past check in time at the hotel." Cian stood and scooped Erin up in his arms, causing her to giggle.

"Oh, no! I won't have it. You'll stay at the family farm. It's me and Ma there only, and the two of us will be here till she's strong enough to go home." I could see the determination in her eyes and the set of her jaw. "Go on with yourself, now and settle in. There are two spare bedrooms upstairs. Erin will fit nicely in my Colleen's old room. She stays in a flat in town. The other room is at the end of the hall. The key will be found under the ceramic mushroom by the garden gnome."

"That's kind of you. It will make helping out with the sheep easier." Kissing her on the cheek, I left with Cian and Erin to "settle in."

Chapter 5
Settling In

"Oh, Mommy, look! I see Gabriel!" Erin's feet pummeled on the back of the seat in front of her, which happened to be mine

"Remember to keep your distance from the donkey. He may love the sheep, but that doesn't mean Gabriel loves you." I shifted in the seat to better see her in the mirror in order to make eye contact.

"Yes, wee lassie. He may see ye as a threat to his sheep."

Gabriel, the donkey, guarded the sheep. His loud, obnoxious bray and aggressive behavior toward would be predators kept the sheep safe—for the most part. He had been raised among the sheep, and saw them as his family. He wouldn't hurt them, and would do what he could to protect them.

"I'll stay far from Gabriel, but maybe he will decide I'm no threat." Erin unclicked her seatbelt as soon as Cian stopped the car. She hopped out, locating the garden gnome and mushroom by the time Cian and I got out to join her.

A chipped green paint graced the solid wood front door. Cian stepped back to let Erin and me enter ahead of him. Inside the two story farmhouse was like stepping back in time. Colleen, grand-dad Irish's youngest sibling, told us the history of the house when we visited it the first time during Erin's birthday trip six months earlier.

My great, great grand-father and his wife lived on the land in a shack while they acquired sheep. Rumor had it he won the majority of his sheep in a game of cards at the local tavern. He even convinced the man he won them from it was his duty to help him build a barn and put up a fence to house the sheep he so carelessly lost to him.

For such a miracle, he probably kissed the Blarney Stone himself. The young couple had land, sheep, and a barn. Eventually, they built the farmhouse—finished just in time to welcome their first child.

I loved the fact that my family had lived in the old farm house ever since, with sheep dotting the land. Being in the house grand-dad Irish grew up in made me feel closer to him, almost as if his presence had remained.

Pictures of him and his four younger siblings lined the hall. Walking past the pictures toward the bedrooms, I touched a photo of grand-dad Irish saying a silent "I love you."

"Mommy, is this my room?" Erin pushed open the door, revealing a turquoise room with purple curtains and black curly scrolls painted as a border. Rushing in and jumping up on the twin bed, she patted the dark purple spread. "Mommy, I love this room! If my Iris were here, we could stay forever."

"We won't be staying that long, Lassie." Cian set her bag down at the foot of the bed.

"But we will be staying long enough to unpack your things. So, get started on that while your da and I do the same. This used to be young Colleen's room. She'll be glad to know you like it."

Opening the door at the end of the hall, I walked into a room with sparse decorations. Besides the queen-sized bed, a night stand and trunk lay at the foot of the bed. Nothing hung on the walls. What the room lacked in décor, the windows made up for. One wall held nothing but paned windows looking out over the green pastures, dotted with sheep. Downstairs all the curtains had been left closed. Up here, the pulled back drapes allowed the clear blue sky to infuse the pale blue room with a soft glow. Cian and I looked at each other at the same time. Dropping the bags I fell onto the bed with my husband, being careful not to put my shoes on the cover.

"Are ye as tired as I?" Cian turned his head to me. I nodded without speaking. Turning on his side, he brushed a strand of hair off my forehead. "This must be hard on you—surrounded by memories of your grand-dad, losing his brother and possibly his sister as well."

My heart skipped a beat at seeing the love and concern in his eyes. "It's a little like losing more of grand-dad. Your understanding means the world to me."

He lifted my chin and touched his lips with mine. Relaxing into the tender kiss, I ran my hands through his wavy, blond hair. Drawn into his arms, he held me until Erin burst into the room and jumped on top of us.

Cian grabbed her feet, tickling her bare soles. I helped him in the torment, blowing raspberries on her stomach. Whatever did we do for entertainment before Erin?

Late the next morning, sunrays shone in between the clouds drifting across the sky. I reached up to unclip another towel from the line and dropped it in the basket. Erin ran by singing some silly song.

Cian's mother, Ina, had hung clothes on a line while Cian and I chased each other under the clouds and over the green hills. The thought brought a smile to my heart that showed on my face. Oh, it felt good to be back in Ireland.

Dropping the last towel in the basket, I scanned the vicinity for Erin. I spied her standing on the wooden gate that opened to the sheep pasture.

"Be mindful of the donkey!" I called out to her. She waved in response.

The sound of a car moving up the gravel drive made me turn. Behind the wheel, Cian pulled the vehicle up to the side yard. He had gone to the market to get us something to eat for lunch and dinner. I rushed to help him carry in the groceries. Together, we took them into the kitchen that looked out the back of the house.

"Looks like a fine day for a picnic. I'll find a quilt while you make some sandwiches?" He wrapped his arms around me and nuzzled my neck. I kept washing the strawberries at the sink.

"I love that idea! Look in the trunk in our room. I leaned into him once more before he went to locate a quilt for our impromptu picnic.

With our sandwiches eaten, the three of us lay on our backs looking up into the branches of the plum tree we spread our quilt under. The breeze sent a sudden chill across my body.

"Do you hear that?" I sat up, listening.

Cian sat up too. "What?" He cocked his head.

"A siren! I hear it, Mommy! Look, it's turning up the drive!"

My shifting gaze turned to Cian for only a moment before I stood. "Stay here, Erin, and don't let the quilt blow away.

My ever attentive husband, Cian, walked with me to the front of the house in time to greet a police car followed by Jewel's. Behind her vehicle a hearse had stopped.

Jewell climbed out of her car at seeing us, her eyes red and puffy. "Sorry, I am for not calling you, everything happened so fast. I couldn't think of anything beyond getting them home." She shook her head as if to clear a fog.

"Them?" Cian spoke what I feared.

"Yes. Them. Knowing I am burying uncle Kyle tomorrow, they took care of mother posthaste so we can hold a double wake."

"Double wake?" I held my breath and grabbed Cian's hand.

"Oh, mercy! Sorry, I am to surprise you like this. Mother died yesterday at sunset. She never regained consciousness after the stroke. She just slipped away."

Men from the funeral home carried the coffins into the house. Cian held the door for them. A rising numbness almost rooted me to the spot but I managed to embrace Jewell. Comfort the only thing I could give for such a terrible outcome of losing her uncle and mother so close together— the last two siblings of grand-dad Irish's generation.

The rest of the day and next morning, a flurry of activity turned the house into a bustle of chaos to get the residence ready for the wake. Near and far neighbors brought over sandwiches, salads and desserts. I made Jewel lay down for a bit and had Cian help me make tea and lemonade. Young Colleen, with Erin's help, filled plastic cups with ice.

People who had grown up with Jewel, or knew great uncle Kyle or Colleen through church or the sheep business, filed in and out over lunch. Most of them shared a memory or two of Kyle or Colleen. They nibbled on sandwiches and consumed the salads. The laughter from the stories eased my heavy heart.

After a couple of hours the window left open for the spirits to depart was shut, to keep them from re-entering. I hung back and squeezed Cian's hand, watching the workers load the coffins back into the hearse. All who could, followed the hearse to the cemetery where the other members of the Dooley family lay buried.

CHAPTER 6
The Erin Tree

"Beautiful house you have here, Jewel," I said walking into the kitchen for coffee. Jewel stood at the farmhouse sink washing plums. Ever since the funeral she bustled around the house, inside and out, from task to task, like a honey bee flying from flower to flower in the garden.

"Ah yes, it has its charm for sure, if you ignore the faulty wiring and outdated plumbing." Her head, bent over the task at hand, disregarded the view of green pastures dotted with sheep filling the window in front of her. "During your visit I'll be sure to dig out the old pictures of the house and family. There'll be some of your grand-da as a young-un for sure. You favor the family, you do. I see it in your smile—even hear it in your laugh." Drying her hands on the apron hanging about her trim waist, she turned to lean against the sink.

"I hate for you to go to any trouble, but I'd love to see them. Is there anything I can do to help you with the plums?

Cian is out checking the fences for any openings, and Erin went with him, hoping to get a glimpse of Gabriel. My time is my own."

Smiling, I held out my empty hands to indicate I had nothing better to do than help her.

"Well, in that case, you can cut an X on the top of each plum. I'll blanch five at a time after you cut the X's. Then, I'll put them in a bowl of ice water for thirty seconds. You can take them out of the ice water and both of us can peel their skins off. The X makes it easier to peel the skin back." Jewel handed me a paring knife.

I might have just gotten in over my head, but opened a drawer and

25

pulled out an apron with a red and green apple print. Without getting the cup of coffee I'd entered the kitchen for in the first place, I dove into the task.

From time to time I glanced out the window wondering how things were going with Cian and Erin.

"Woohoo, faster Da, faster!"

At his daughter's command, Cian gassed the engine, speeding down the slope and across the creek in order to spray water over the truck. Erin's head bumped the ceiling of the old farm truck, but she still squealed in delight at the water sprinkling her through the open window.

The truck lurched at his downshift, but a quick press of the pedal to the floor threw Erin against the seat back. The lower gear helped the truck climb the opposite bank.

Cian believed in taking the time to make a chore fun, especially when it involved his daughter. The two of them had spent the morning driving the fence perimeter, stopping to make reinforcements or repairs where necessary. Erin wasn't exactly the most helpful. She ran around picking wild flowers or blowing dandelions at every section he stopped at.

"Would ye look at that great big tree with the low branches? I think it's time ye learned to climb a tree." Cian stopped the truck and helped Erin hop out. He wrapped his arms around the lowest branch and walked his legs up the trunk until he could swing one leg over the branch. He pulled himself around to the topside. Before he sat up, he reached down for Erin. "Can ye reach me hand, lassie?"

"I think so." Erin stretched for him, her little body straining to get taller. Cian grasped her hand and pulled her up into the tree.

The moment he sat up with her she said, "Can I go higher, Da?"

"Put your foot in the V of the tree right there to reach the next branch. Watch what you're doing now. Your ma would not be pleased with me if I let ye fall out of a tree." Cian held her hand, helping her edge past him to get where the branches split on the trunk.

At the V of the tree Erin stopped. "Da, my name is carved in the tree!"

"What? Ye sure it's your name?" Standing, Cian craned his neck to see the carving Erin ran her hand over.

Someone had carved, Liam & Erin were here 8-1952.

"Well, lassie, Liam is your great grandfather's name. He probably carved that as a boy. He must've had a friend, or maybe a cousin named Erin."

"I declare this tree the Erin Tree. It belongs to me since it has my name on it." She made the declaration with her head held high.

Her sassiness always made him laugh. Cian helped her out of the tree. "Let's go tell your ma what we found."

"Go over lots of bumps and hills real fast on the way back. Okay, Da?"

Such an incorrigible daughter he had. Cian grinned and watched her seatbelt click in place.

"Whew. Canning is more work than I realized." I untied my apron and used it to wipe my forehead. I heard Cian and Erin enter the front door. "Just follow the sweet, tangy smell to the kitchen!" I called out to them.

"Look what the cat drug in—just in time to carry these jars to the cellar for me." Jewel untied her apron and motioned to the jars lining the counter. "Irelyn helped me make plum jelly this morning."

"Ye did this, Irelyn?" Cian's eyebrows raised. "Did ye write down the directions so ye can do it at home?"

"Don't look so surprised, mister, or I may give you a reason." I gave him a playful swat with the apron I held in my hands.

Before the apron could fall back to my side, he crossed the room and lifted me into the air. He planted a kiss next to my mouth the moment my feet touched the floor. "Mmm…" He licked his lips. "I love plum jelly."

"You and Erin go wash up while I set lunch out." Jewel opened the fridge and took out the leftover Shepherd's Pie we ate for dinner the night before. "Irelyn, do you mind helping me with one more thing?"

"Of course, I'll slice some bread and get out the butter."

Jewel's mother, Colleen, taught her womanly virtue required her to have homemade bread available for each meal. Jewel shared with me she didn't feel the same but had grown used to having it, and the aroma smelled like home to her. I had to admit, warm bread with soft Irish butter dressed up leftovers quite nicely.

"Did Erin tell ye she found her name carved in a tree today?" Cian said to me, pausing from reading his Clive Cussler book. He often read while waiting for me to get ready for bed.

"No. Did you carve it for her?" I pulled my nightgown over my head, enjoying the way the silk slid down my back.

"No, I didn't. It's dated August 1952, and it has your grand-dad's name and Erin. Do ye think he had a friend named Erin, or maybe a cousin?"

By the time I turned around, he had abandoned the book and only watched me. "Wow, that's some coincidence. I'd like to see this carving. 1952 is the year he went to the States. I'll ask Jewel if she knows anything about a friend or cousin named Erin. She promised to dig out the old family photos for us to look through while we're here. Speaking of Erin—she asked me something strange tonight when I put her to bed." Sliding under the cover, I snuggled up to Cian.

"Hmm?" He nuzzled my neck, leaving a trail of kisses.

My focus tried to waver, but I fought through. "She asked me if… oh…" I lifted my chin to give him better access.

"Yes?" He continued the onslaught with his lips.

I took a deep breath. "…if a butterfly can fly over the ocean." The words came out in a rush.

"Our wee lassie's curiosity knows no bounds." His exploring hands destroyed the little bit left of my will. I gave up on words—immersing into the pleasure.

Chapter 7
The Devil Seeks
Antigua 1669

The bright sunshine of Antigua beat down on Ms. Calleah's cool hut. The sugar apples and periwinkles needed picking so she had no choice but to pull her wide brimmed hat low on her brow and head out to the grove.

Bent over, she picked the purple flowers, picturing how the cut stems, boiled in water, would help with the swelling of ankles and extremities. As an Obeah, people came from all around the island to her for various remedies.

Ms. Calleah helped those she could, but her true purpose was to help Wendy, the sugar plantation owner's crippled daughter. She had cared for the motherless girl since Wendy's birth. The hard labor to bring her into the world had left her mother dead soon after. Even in the advanced year of 1642 women still died in childbirth.

The squalling child had latched onto her pinky and eagerly sucked. From that moment on Ms. Calleah lost her heart.

Wendy grew into a lovely young lady, married with children of her own. Old Mr. Kincaid, the plantation owner had long since passed. Wendy and her husband ran the sugar mill these days.

Upon Wendy's insistence, Ms. Calleah "retired." If it were up to her, she'd still be watching after Wendy's young lad, Christopher, the toddling girl, Aisley, and young master, Benjamin. What did young'uns playing house know about raising children? Although she kept busy mixing herbs and such for the people of the plantation, she felt her true purpose had been denied her.

29

A periwinkle landed on her foot, soft as a feather's touch. She noticed the basket rim overflowed with flowers. She moved on to the trees, filling her shoulder bag with sugar apples. The juice pressed from the fruit helped with coughs, flu, fever, and upset stomachs.

Satisfied with the day's bounty, and her damp dress pressing against her back, she determined to walk down to shell cove to cool her tired feet on the way to her hut.

Emerging from the path into the cove, a moaning sound caught her ear. Maybe one of the slaves cut their foot or got stung by a jellyfish. She set her basket on a rock and let the shoulder bag slip down her arm, scanning the cove—ready to help.

Off to the left lay a man on his side writhing in pain. She Knelt beside him and turned him over, supporting his weight as she did so. Beneath him, blood stained the sand. The sight of his face made her eyes grow wide and her mouth drop open.

"Cal? Cal, is it you?" She shook his shoulders, her gaze roaming his body for the source of blood. "Oh, merciful Lord in Heaven, it is you! What happened?" She took off her apron, removed the knife protruding from his abdomen, and pressed the bundled apron to the wound. Cal cried out when she pressed on the wound but she knew of no other way to stop the flow of blood.

"Irelyn. She did this." His breathing shallow and irregular, he let out a hiss. "They must pay." Anger burned in his eyes.

"Ssh. Shush now, don't talk. Hold my apron to the wound. I'm going to get help to carry you back to the hut. I'll fix you right up." Miss Calleah hadn't seen her brother Cal since he insisted she help him go forward in time to follow Cian, about twelve years earlier under a Blue Moon. She doubted her scheming brother would survive this latest escapade. Nonetheless, she hurried to the plantation as fast as her weary legs allowed, uttering prayers and intonations along the way.

Cal's blood loss left him drifting in and out of consciousness for several days. Calleah kept him sedated. Every time he awoke she spoon fed him soup.

On his cot another bout of moaning and thrashing came. Calleah rushed to calm him. He grabbed her by the shoulders, glaring into her eyes. "You're my sister. My death must be avenged! You must!"

"You are no ghost. There is no death to avenge. Rest, brother. You are back home in your own time, where you belong. No one will harm you here." She pulled out of his grasp and went to get a wet cloth so he wouldn't see the distress etched on her face.

She should have never helped him follow Cian into the future. She had known then no good would come of it. But never one to be content with his circumstances, he had grown into a greedy, self-seeking, despicable man. He followed Cian to the future scheming to steal his coins.

Once he disappeared under the blue moon, she had hoped it would be the last she saw him, but here he lay dying. And as Cal said, he didn't deserve to be stabbed by Irelyn while he slept. She smoothed the worry out of her face and turned back to Cal, laying the cloth on his fevered skin.

His tear-filled eyes pleaded with her. "Don't let her come after me. Please. She commands spirits. Stop her. Avenge me!" The more he spoke, the less coherent and sane he sounded. However, in this state he reminded her of the scared little boy she had spent many nights comforting after they'd been sold into slavery.

"Ssh. Ssh now. Don't fret. Calleah always takes care of you, don't she?" She continued wiping his heated skin with the rag.

"You'll avenge me, won't you, Callie?" he whispered before sinking into slumber.

"Brother, why don't you get up and come out to enjoy the sunshine? Two years be too long to lie around every day. Your wound long since healed. What ails you?" Ms. Calleah wiped sweat off her neck with a colorful handkerchief before tying it around her head.

Mumbling unintelligible words, Cal turned over with his back to the room.

Ms. Calleah could do no more than to let him be, so she left. She sat under the tree outside the hut to shuck corn for their meal. Pulling the husks off the corn didn't do much to help her thoughts about her brother.

She had been caring for him for two years now. The only thing ailing him seemed to be his mind. Anytime his words turned coherent, he told wild stories about the future. Traveling for no good cause probably led to his torment. Also, according to Cal, Cian and Irelyn treated him unjustly, leading to Irelyn stabbing him in his sleep. She had a hard time believing Irelyn would do such a thing, but the last time she saw her, Irelyn hadn't been older than four or five years old. People change—yes they do. Not always for good.

"That ol' cunning devil, he go round this earth seeking. Yes, he do. He go here and there—seeking. Like a hungry lion, he is. Irelyn must've not resisted the devious one. My brother lying here suffering from her misdeeds is evidence of the evil in her. I too suffer from her misdeeds." Ms. Calleah didn't bother to mask her frown. She let it deepen, etching itself on her face. "Cal's right bout one thing—something must be done bout her. Yes, yes, indeed."

CHAPTER 8
Storms

Feather thin clouds streaked across the morning sky. It promised to be a beautiful day. I waved to Cian on his way to the barn and called for Erin. Her lack of answer had me jogging upstairs to find her. No point wasting my breath and disturbing Jewell by hollering. I found her in the bedroom she'd been given.

"There you are. Didn't you hear me call you?"

Erin sat on the floor, drawing in her journal.

"What are you drawing, honey?" I tilted my head to get a better view.

"I'm drawing a picture of Iris to show cousin Jewell."

"I'm sorry you miss your pony. Jewell will love seeing a picture of Iris." Bending over, I drug her shoes out from under the bed.

"I wish she could've come, but I don't think she would've liked the airplane ride at all. I brought my favorite rock instead. Are we going somewhere?" She reached out and took the shoes from me.

"Yep, so get your shoes on. We're going with Jewell to the Market." I tried convincing her it would be fun by smiling ear to ear.

"Mommy, noooo. Please, may I stay with Da?" Erin crossed her arms and stuck out her bottom lip. "I'm a good helper, Da says so. Please? Pretty please?" Her clasped hands under her chin made her look like a precious angel.

"Oh, all right. Your da is in the barn. Stay out of his way, and mind what he says." I preferred to go to the market without her anyway. She had a habit of adding things to the buggy every time I looked the other way. "Put your journal away and go to the barn once you have your shoes on." I narrowed my eyes at this last bit.

The child had a bad habit of slipping out of her shoes at every opportunity. She even went so far as to toss them out the car window from her car seat at two years old. I shook my head, yet smiled at the memory, going back down to the kitchen to wait for Jewell.

The top of the Dutch door stood open. The lovely view beyond held me captive. At the sound of Erin flying in I put my hand on the bottom part of the door to hold it shut. "Slow down, little one. Don't I get a kiss or a hug?"

Her arms wrapped around my waist. "You get both!"

I stooped over so she could kiss my cheek. Then she was out the door, running to the barn. Drying my cheek from her moist smack, the unicorns on her shoes looked as if they aided in her swift escape.

"The storm clouds blew in so fast. The sun shone when we left, and we've only been gone just over an hour." Jewell stepped harder on the gas, speeding the car around the hills. "I hope we get back and unload the groceries before those black clouds let loose."

"I'll text Cian so he'll be ready to come out and help us get the groceries in quickly." My shoulder hit the door at another of Jewell's sharp turns.

Flying leaves and twigs blown from the trees crossed the road and the car. Lightning streaked across the sky, followed by a clap of thunder.

Jewell turned between the old stone pillars marking the entrance to the Dooley sheep farm. She drove as close to the back door as possible before stepping on the brake.

Jumping down off the porch, Cian didn't waste any time getting the groceries in the kitchen.

"I'm glad you're back." He gave me a peck on the lips. Looking at Jewell, he said, "Almost all the expecting ewes and ewes with lambs are gathered in the barn. There still be several to round up. One of ye ladies want to lend me a hand?"

"Be done quicker with all of us, it will." Jewell shook out a plastic rain bonnet and tied it under her chin. She winked at Cian and me. "Wouldn't like to dampen my curls."

It took only a moment to pull my hair into a quick ponytail, to keep the wind from whipping it in my eyes. "Let's go. Best to let Erin stay where she is. I'd rather her not be out in the storm."

"Agreed." Cian led the way to the enclosed field that held the ewes with lambs and those expecting.

Jewell and I held hands, the strong winds buffeting our efforts to run. Reaching the field, the heavy rain drops pelted us in a steady rhythm, increasing the urgency.

The flashing lightning and booming thunder didn't help Cian's fumbling fingers with the gate. Sheets of rain turned the storm into a torrential downpour.

The gate swung open and we each rushed toward a bleating bundle of white in the dark. Cian and Jewell ushered their sheep toward the barn. I ran to the far corner where a lamb stood trying his best to shelter against the fence.

I scooped him up, my arms wrapping around his front and back legs. Expecting him to be heavy, I over compensated. My back arched and my feet slipped out from under me on the slick grass. Landing on my bottom with the lamb in my lap winded me. I made no immediate move to get up, even with the wet seeping through my jeans. Cian's long strides to reach me made my heart swell with pride. My knight in shining armor. He's coming to help me up.

"Irelyn, this be no time to cuddle lambs." He lifted the lamb out of my arms and turned to the barn.

Left to fend for myself I didn't have time to be indignant, not with the rain and lightning showing no signs of stopping in the growing darkness. I scrambled up and ran after him.

Inside the barn all the ewes with lambs and the ones expecting had all been accounted for.

"We don't have to worry about the rest. They'll find shelter under trees and bushes," Jewell said heading back to the house. "Oh heavens above, appears the electricity is off at the house. I swear, every time we get a heavy rain or a big wind it goes out, it does."

The weather swirling around us doubled my worries at her words.

She reached out and touched my shoulder. "Don't worry, I have plenty of candles, and it never stays out for long."

"Erin!" I said. She would be terrified in the dark house alone. Cian took off running for the house. I wasn't far behind him.

"Erin!" Each of us hollered the moment we entered the back door.

"We're here, honey. Where are you?" Not hearing anything, I headed for the stairs.

"Lassie," Cian said, coming up next to me with a flashlight in his hands. "I know you're a brave one, but where are ye?" He shone the light down the hall.

"Erin?" I opened the door to her bedroom. Cian shone the light inside.

Maybe she hid from us because we left her in the house alone. I tiptoed to the bed, throwing up the bed skirt. "Boo!"

Cian's scan under the bed with the light showed nothing but a dust bunny or two. Holding a finger to his lips, he motioned me to the closet. I threw open the door and once again yelled, "Boo!"

The closet did not reveal our precocious child. Cian and I looked at each other.

"Where is she?" I said almost in unison with Cian.

"I haven't seen her since Jewell and I left for the market."

"What do ye mean? Ye took her to the market." Cian scratched his head, throwing haphazard beams of light around the room.

My skin prickled, causing the hairs on the back of my neck to stand. "Cian, I did not take her to the market. She wanted to stay and help you. The last time I saw her, she was headed out to the barn to join you." I rubbed my arms and inhaled several times in an effort to remain calm.

"Well, there's the pickle. Our lassie never came into the barn. I haven't seen her since breakfast. Mayhap she went to look for Gabriel instead. We'll find her, love. Don't fret."

The final thread of my control broke, the battle for calm surrendered. Words spilled from my mouth, my voice rising with each one uttered. "She's scared, scared of storms. I shouldn't have let her stay. She didn't want to go." My heaving chest sucked in copious amounts of air.

Cian gripped both my arms in his strong, capable hands. "Look at me." The flashlight rolled across the wood floor, sounding like distant thunder. "We will find our wee lassie. Ye know how adventurous she is. She probably wondered off and is hiding 'til the storm blows over. Do ye hear me?" Lifting my chin, he gazed into my eyes.

The assurity I saw there gave me the strength to nod my head though tears rolled down my face.

Outside, thunder boomed. I straightened my spine and dried my eyes. "Let's go find our baby girl."

CHAPTER 9
The Search

The thought of her lost in the dark, alone, and scared of the storm was too much to bear. It kept me going, searching for Erin all night.

With Cian at my side, we sought places of shelter from the storm, expecting to find her well before daybreak.

"Irelyn, there be the tree Erin and I climbed. The one that bears her name. Maybe she's there."

The branches of the elderly tree with her name carved on it blew in the wind, but it's swaying form wasn't sheltering our Erin.

We hunted down Gabriel. She loved the donkey and might've been concerned for his safety in the storm. Gabriel stood with a large number of sheep in an outcropping of boulders and bushes, sheltering from the wind and slashing rain—but no Erin.

Following the fenceline, we walked around the perimeter of the land. In every shed we looked and called her name.

My voice grew so hoarse I could no longer shout. I stumbled onward despite my exhaustion.

"It's okay, me dear." Cian caught me, helping me and my wobbly legs to stay upright. "Let's get ye back to the house and call the police."

My body could go no further so I agreed. Even the sky seemed to consent to the decision, ceasing its downpour and harsh winds.

The sun broke over the horizon, ushering in our trudge through the backyard gate. With Cian's help I removed my rain boots then helped him do the same. We left them on the step and entered the door. The aroma of coffee brewing and biscuits in the oven did not offer its usual comfort.

"From the looks of you, I assume you didn't find her?" The hopeful expression on Jewell's face fell. She turned her back to us to remove biscuits from the oven. "Sit yourself down while I pour you a cuppa. After you get a quick bite, you can go take a warm shower."

"Many thanks to ye, Jewell." Cian rubbed a trembling hand across his face.

I dropped into a kitchen chair, burying my head in my arms on the table to utter a prayer for Erin's safety. How could this be happening?

"While the two of you shower and dress, why don't I call some neighbors to come over and help search? Maybe you could get some rest and let them search for a bit." Jewell set a warm biscuit and a cup of coffee in front of me on the table, and then carried the same over for Cian.

"No! We'll keep searching." Cian shook his head as if to clear it. "I'm sorry, Jewell. Don't mean to snap at ye."

"Any help at all would be welcomed, Jewell, but I don't think either of us could rest until she's found." Just lifting my head to speak required enormous energy. I buried it once more.

"Oh, bless your souls. I take no offense, Cian. I understand. Down the coffee and take a bit of a biscuit before you trot upstairs for a warm shower. It'll do you good, sure it will. Go on." I raised my head high enough to take a gulp of coffee but left the biscuit alone.

Cian slathered butter on his and devoured it in two bites. Seeing the butter drip from the side of his biscuit made my stomach grumble so loud Cian slid the butter to me.

"Eat, Irelyn love, or I'll have to worry about ye as well as our lassie." His words held a sense I couldn't deny. I dutifully ate the biscuit. It quieted the grumble in my stomach, but the normalcy of eating felt wrong with my world in such turmoil.

Cian held his hand out to help me up. In silence we lumbered to the stairs, holding onto each other's hand like a life line.

"Irelyn, do ye hear that? Sounds like a horde of people downstairs." Cian sat on the edge of the bed, tightening the laces on his hiking boots.

Sticking my head out the bathroom door, I stopped brushing my teeth to cock an ear to listen. Loud sounds, like a throng of people, had me raising an eyebrow in question. Hope blossomed deep within, filling me with new energy. "We're going to find her," I said with fierce conviction.

"Of course we are, darling." Cian kissed my forehead and led the way downstairs into a host of neighbors gathered in the old farmhouse kitchen. Spotting Jewell's daughter, Colleen, in the crowd, I hastened over and hugged her for coming.

"Sure, I came. Can't let harm come to our wee cousin, now can we?" Colleen spoke with a smile, but I noticed her eyes glistened with unshed tears.

Standing on the stairs, Cian addressed Jewell's neighbors. "We thank ye mightily for the time and diligence you're lending our family." Cian visibly swallowed a lump in his throat. "Our Erin is lost. She could be scared and hiding or she may've strayed onto a neighboring property. She's been missing since before the storm, so she may be hurt. Pair up and let's find her soon, aye?"

Some in the crowd nodded and clapped while others called out encouraging sentiments. I stepped forward and raised my hand to gain the crowd's attention.

"She's wearing a white t-shirt with a pony on it and dark purple pants. Thank you all for your help. Please find our baby girl." A tear escaped to run down my face and drip off my chin.

Sunlight streamed in from the back door Jewell opened. "I'll have lunch ready for everyone at noon. In between now and lunch, Colleen will drive around in the truck with lemonade and water."

Colleen's smile confirmed the pronouncement.

Everyone filed out the door talking amongst themselves. I turned big eyes to Cian.

"She'll be found before lunch, Cian. She has to!" I gripped his sleeve in my fist.

"Yes, yes. We will fix her a grilled cheese sandwich piled high with gooey cheese the way our lassie likes it." Taking me by the hand, he led me outside to join the search.

Every volunteer left their muddy shoes on the porch and straggled into the kitchen for lunch. The somber mood increased with each pair who entered with no news of our precious Erin. Cian's tightening grip on my hand turned my fingers numb.

Jewell passed out plates with sandwiches, chips, and grapes to the returned searchers. They ate, conversing amongst themselves in hushed voices. One team had yet to return. I grew tired of watching the minutes on the clock move past noon and the excruciating wait for the door to open to reveal Erin in the arms of the last team. Squeezing Cian's hand, I stood and pulled him with me. Maybe the wait would be more tolerable outside.

I never considered what my parents must have felt when I went missing as a child. Now their overprotective behavior afterwards made sense. Rebelling against their ever watchful eye, I'm sure I caused them much grief.

"Irelyn, they're coming!"

"Do they have her?" I jumped up, straining to see over Cian's shoulder. "Is Erin with them?"

Without a word he sat on the step and put his head in his hands. His body language gave me the answer I didn't want to hear. I sunk to the step beside him and laid my head against his arm, shutting my eyes tight.

"Could this belong to your girl?" A woman held up a small tennis shoe with a pegasus on the side of it. My best friend, Erin's honorary Aunt Sonja, bought the shoes for Erin's birthday.

"Where did you find this?" The moment I took the shoe chills raced across my body. I showed the shoe to Cian.

"Tell us exactly where you found it. There was only one?" Cian said staring at the shoe in my hands.

"Only one," said the man who walked up with the woman. "We were at the back of the property looking along the creek past the fence. The creek rises during a flash flood like we had last night. Can be dangerous. Had a sheep or two carried away by the rush of water last year. Anyhow, Alison here, spotted something between the rocks at the water's edge. How she managed to spy it is beyond me, but I went to check it out. I plucked this here shoe out of the water." His gaze dropped to the ground like he didn't want to make eye contact with me anymore. "I figure it got caught between the rocks, and the other got carried downstream."

I stood with the shoe clenched in my fist. "Are you trying to say my five year old daughter crawled under the barbwire fence, stepped into the stream, and got carried away by the water? Like a sheep? Is that what you're trying to say? Is that what you think happened? Because you found a stinking shoe?" My angry steps moved me closer to the man. Toe-to-toe, I shook the shoe in his face.

His eyes grew wide. "Why no, ma'am, not at all. I'm only saying Alison and I only found one shoe."

"Baby, please, calm down. They're helping us. Now we know our lassie has been to the creek off the property." Cian wrapped his arms around me and pulled me back.

Alison slipped her arm through her bewildered husband's. Passing by, she placed a hand on my arm. "We lost one of our babes. My heart hurts for you both."

Cian's arms tightened around me before I could reply, and they didn't wait around to see if I would. Instead, I turned and buried my head in Cian's shoulder to sob.

"We haven't lost her. We just can't find her. She's out there—our baby girl is out there. I know it!"

"Ssh now, ssh." He ran a trembling hand down my hair over and over, the clutched muddy shoe between us. "You're right, we're going to find her. Our lassie is out there."

Chapter 10
Chasing Butterflies

Erin startled, not remembering right off where she had fallen asleep. In fact, she didn't remember falling to sleep at all. She raised her head, unwrapping her arms from around her knees and heard a donkey braying.

Before the storm Erin had walked into the barn, but heard her da using the saw. He didn't like her around while he cut wood, so not wishing to pester him as her mother admonished, she decided to go say hello to Gabriel.

Sitting on top of the fence, she grew tired of waiting for the donkey to appear. Overhead, swift, dark clouds rolled toward her. She hopped down to return to the barn, but as she neared the large barn doors, a blue butterfly flew right in front of her face.

All thoughts of donkeys, her da, and storms disappeared—chased away by the need to know if the blue butterfly from home followed her to Ireland.

The sky grew darker and darker, but Erin, so bent on catching the butterfly, didn't notice until heavy, fat raindrops started pelting the ground.

A blinding bolt of lightning followed by a crack of thunder jolted her from her chase. Looking around, she wasn't sure where she had ended up.

The rain changed, coming down in sheets. She ran back the way she thought she came. Loud thunder and blinding flashes of lightning heightened her fear. Nothing looked familiar no matter which direction she looked. A large oak tree the only shelter she saw.

She crawled into a hole between the exposed roots of the sprawling oak tree. Hidden beneath the tree, she closed her eyes tight, trying to ignore the tree's moaning with its branches whipping in the howling wind.

When she cracked her eyes open again, she found herself surrounded by dark. Another rub of her eyes and she noticed light shining through a small opening. The light hit her feet and warmed where it touched.

Inside the sunbeam, fairies danced. Her mother said they were dust particles, but her da said they were tiny fairies sent from the heavens to grow and do good deeds on earth. She liked her da's explanation much better.

Not hearing any wind or thunder, Erin climbed out of the hole that sheltered her through the night. She stretched her arms over her head and looked around for Gabriel.

Spotting him in a neighboring field, she tiptoed closer, hoping to avoid sticker burrs. One of her shoes had gotten stuck in the mud by the river the night before, so she had taken the other off too.

"Gabriel! Gabriel!"

Even though Erin called as loud as her scratchy throat allowed, Gabriel wouldn't come to the fence. She put her hands on her hips and frowned. The longer she stared at the donkey, the more she noticed the donkey did not look like Gabriel.

"I'm sorry to holler at you—Momma says it's not polite. You must be a new helper for Gabriel. Well, I must be going home now. Momma and Da are probably looking for me, and I'm awfully hungry." Erin kept her distance from the new donkey and followed the fence—a path that would eventually lead her to the stone house. Not wearing shoes made the going slow and torturous. She stopped numerous times to rest her tender feet from the stones.

Reaching the barn first, Erin poked her head in to peer into the shaded enclosure. "Da, are you in there?" She waited for her da's deep, booming voice—a sure sign he was excited or agitated about some matter. Surely, her spending the night outdoors would bring about such a response, but she didn't hear a sound. She turned toward the house.

"You, there! What business do you have in our barn? Mind yourself and go on about your way." A thin woman in a long dress with an apron tied around her waist stood at the backdoor sweeping the steps.

"I was just looking for my da. My momma says he spends most of his time here in the barn." Erin hopped on one leg to the steps.

"Does she now? Well, I'll be. What are you hopping around like a one legged goose for, lassie?"

"My shoe got stuck in the mud by the creek. I had to walk all the way here barefooted. There sure are a lot of sharp rocks!" Erin winced at another one poking the tender pad of her foot.

"Oh, my heavens! Let me help you inside and I'll doctor you up. You poor thing." The woman wrapped an arm around Erin's waist and carried her up the stairs into the kitchen. "Well, you're a wisp of a girl, now aren't you. Let's see what we can do about that." She set Erin on a metal chair with a yellow padded seat.

Erin frowned, taking in her surroundings. The table and chairs were different, and the curtains too. "Are my momma and da here?" Erin said to the woman setting a plate of warm soda bread and butter on the table in front of her. Her tummy grumbled in anticipation of food. She placed a hand on her stomach.

"I'll not be knowing where your parents be, but they're not here, I assure you."

"Who are you and what are you doing here?" Furrowing her brow, she tried to make sense of the house and farm that looked so much like Cousin Jewell's, yet so different.

"Cora, I am. What is it I do here? Chief bottle washer, cook, laundress, gardener, seamstress, house maid, mother, wife, and nurse to five children to boot." Cora pulled up one of the yellow padded chairs next to Erin and patted her knee asking for her foot.

Erin lifted her foot to Cora's knee. Cora took great care in cleaning her cut foot. Erin started in on the soda bread with much eagerness. Engrossed in smearing butter over the raisin filled bread, she paid no mind to the salve Cora applied to her cut.

"There now, all better. Let's have your name, little one." Cora leaned back in the chair and smiled.

"My name's Er..." She stifled a great big yawn. "Erin." Her head seemed so heavy, she couldn't stop it from nodding. Staying out all night through the storm had worn her out.

Cora took her hand and led her into the next room to a green couch. "Rest your eyes here for a bit. I'll see about finding your ma and da."

Erin nodded and curled up on the couch—asleep in no time at all.

Cora's heart melted, noticing how much the girl looked like her own offspring. Erin's nose, eyes, even the shape of her mouth all testified to the chance of her being kin. Raising her apron to pat her eyes, she thought, Lord, it's time to have a talk with that oldest boy of ours. Time for him to step up and be a man.

CHAPTER 11
Always Something
Antigua 1669

Clouds moved quickly across the cerulean blue sky, covering the sun. The white sheet Wendy hung snapped in the sudden breeze. Maizie, the young woman that helped with the household chores and children when needed, looked up at the dark clouds.

"Missus, I thinks you best be gettin' inside." Maizie handed Wendy her walking canes and picked up the empty bamboo basket.

"Don't give me that look, Maizie. I will hang my own laundry on the line if I wish to." She looked at Maizie with a half smile and said, "I'd think less work would make you happy. But you're right, it feels like a storm is brewing. Have Jeremiah bring my mare to the step, please. I want to check on Ms. Calleah before the storm. I haven't seen her in much too long."

Wendy leaned on the porch column by the carriage step of her home while she waited for Jeremiah to appear with her horse. She laid her canes against her to tie a handkerchief over her head and around her long brunette hair to keep the wind from blowing it every direction.

She had been meaning to go see about Ms. Calleah for a while, but something always came up with the children or the plantation. Truth be told, she regretted insisting that Ms. Calleah retire. No one knew and understood her like Ms. Calleah, but Wendy noticed her slowing down, and holding her back with a pained expression on her face. If Ms. Calleah hurt, keeping her around to help her with the children would have been selfish of her. Though she sure did miss her, as did the children. Next time she'd take the children with her to visit, not enough time today what with the storm rolling in…

Always something. Isn't that the usual way of it?

The familiar trot of her sweet mare made her turn. She smiled at Jeremiah who rode upon her horse. Jeremiah and Maizie had been at the Windy Palm Plantation for several years. Wendy's father, Mr. Kincaid, the original plantation owner, had been a kind man. Slaves worked the plantation but were treated well—more like indentured servants. Slaves at other farms and sugar mills didn't fare so well.

Arriving at the hut, Wendy tied up the horse under darkening skies and called out. "Ms. Calleah!"

No one answered. She stuck her head in the door to make sure Calleah wasn't inside. Finding it empty, she took a moment to peruse the interior. Although she found it clean and neat, the abysmal living conditions of Ms. Calleah and her brother shamed her. Bamboo mats covered the dirt floor, with only one bed. Ms. Calleah's caregiver instincts, almost ensured Cal would be the one who slept in comfort. Ducking her head back out of the small hut, she determined to search out her old nanny.

A tree stump at the corner of the hut presented the perfect lift she required to remount. Bringing her horse near, she heard voices. She dropped the reins and grasped her walking canes, heading to the rear of the hut. Ms. Calleah had an outdoor kitchen of sorts there.

Getting closer, she realized the sound wasn't speaking but chanting. Intrigued, but not wanting to interrupt, Wendy stayed behind the corner of the hut.

"Oh, dark spirits that roam, those that time does not hold. You search, I know, for ones to be your own. There is one, I know who yearns to be your own. Help is all you need do, a small push is all required of you. Dark ones you are, and dark too she be. With your aid I'll make her rue the day. Irelyn be her name, find her for me." Calleah repeated the menacing plea over and over.

Wendy leaned her head against the hut. She couldn't believe her ears. Surely, this couldn't be her Ms. Calleah who spoke like this.

Taking a deep breath, she peeked around the corner. There sat Ms. Calleah in front of a smoldering mound of what looked to be herbs and the remains of a small animal. Charred meat and skin still clung to the bones. Her head bent over the mound, she rocked side to side with her arms held out beside her, palms down. Next to Calleah sat her brother Cal, with his palms down to the earth. He too moved to the sinister petition, as if its tempo pulsed through his body. His fingers curled in over and over again, raking through the dirt at his sister's chanting.

One heavy raindrop plopped on Wendy's forehead, reminding her of why she came. Ms. Calleah certainly seemed well enough. She made her way back to the horse and galloped home. She didn't know what to make of the chilling chant she heard Ms. Calleah uttering. Why on God's green earth would Ms. Calleah wish harm to Irelyn? How could it even be possible to achieve such a thing with Irelyn being in a future time?

Cian and Irelyn had been Wendy's playmates as children. Wendy believed Irelyn had been lost during a typhoon as a child. Years later, after Cian lost his parents, Ina and Brian, he told her the truth about Irelyn being sent back to her own time with the help of Ms. Calleah during a Blue Moon. He had said he intended to join her in the future. Wendy thought he'd gone mad from grief—until she witnessed him disappear with her own eyes.

Wendy bolted home through the now pouring rain, her whirring mind bent on figuring out how to protect Cian and Irelyn from danger.

CHAPTER 12
What Do Birds Know of Grief?

T he screen door slammed, sounding Cian's return from the
fields. Sitting down at the kitchen table, he proceeded to tell
Jewell about the work he'd done and the repairs he'd yet to do.
"Cian, I told you not to worry yourself about the farm." She set a
cup of black coffee in front of him. "Daniel, across the way, said he'd
come by to repair the fence the felled tree damaged. I do appreciate you
cutting the tree up and removing it." She laid a hand on Cian's shoulder
and squeezed. "You have more than enough on your plate right now."

"It helps to stay busy. Every morning and every evening I drive
along the creek bank looking for our lassie—hoping I don't find her
wee body—" An anguished sob escaped, preventing him from saying
more. He inhaled deeply to fight back his emotions. Jewel's willingness
to allow him to sit in silence and sip his coffee helped.

"I'm going up to check on Irelyn." Pushing back the chair, he
rose and turned toward the stairs, taking them two at a time. At the
bedroom door he hesitated, giving himself time to compose himself.
Irelyn needed him to be strong and positive.

With one more mental reminder to be strong, he opened the door.
The sight of Irelyn caused a physical ache in his heart. His dear wife
lay on her side, curled inward. Her beautiful, long, red curls looked like
she hadn't combed them, or washed them for that matter, in a week.

She clutched Erin's princess dress to her chest. Her opened eyes
didn't move, a frozen stare that didn't seem to be taking in anything.
His biggest fear, other than not finding Erin alive, was losing Irelyn to
grief. Even worse, he feared Irelyn blamed him for Erin's disappearance.

He approached the bed with slow careful steps, willing her to look up at him with a smile, albeit a sad one. He would give anything for some small sign she held no ill feelings for him—but no sign came. He still laid down behind her, cradling her in his strong arms. Cian brushed the mussed curls away from her wet face.

"A mhuirnin, darling, ye need to come downstairs and eat. Ye may feel better out in the sunshine. Please, love, for me? I'm going to start the shower for ye. You'll feel better. Then we'll ride into town to speak to the garda—ask if they've found anything." Cian kissed the back of her head before rising to start the shower. Her grief reminded him of his mother's, after his younger sister, Erin, died from fever. His ma lost the light in her eyes. Cian had done his best to make his ma smile, but it never reached her eyes. He felt powerless then, just as he did now.

A bird hopped across the hood of the rental car in the drive. At one time I would've been intrigued with the bird's movements and whistled to it, trying to get it to respond. But today was not a normal day. There would never be another normal day for me. So, instead of interacting with a silly bird who knew nothing of my grief, I sat in the car waiting for Cian.

I didn't want to get up. I didn't want to shower, or eat. A black cloud of despair, anger, frustration, and defeat engulfed me. I wanted to be left alone. I wanted to lie there in bed, not eating until I died. Yes, I wanted to die. Maybe then, I'd see my baby girl.

Living without her demanded more strength than I could muster. Besides, it was my fault. What kind of mother allowed her young daughter to stay home with her dad, without making sure her dad knew? I didn't even watch Erin go into the barn. How could Cian stand to look at me? I couldn't bring myself to look him in the eye—afraid of the loathing I'd see lurking there.

Cian wouldn't allow me to stay in bed. I went along with his plan today because he said we'd drive to town to speak to the police about the "recovery" search, as they called it, for Erin. I jumped at the driver side door opening. The bird took flight as well. Cian slid in to sit behind the wheel.

"Buckle up and we're off." He reached over and squeezed my hand.

Neither of us spoke during the drive to the station. I pretended to take in the scenery, keeping my head turned to the window. My hands clenched in my lap.

Pulling up under a tree, Cian put the car in park. He took off his seatbelt and turned to me. I would have kept my gaze averted but he put his hand under my chin and turned my face to his.

"Let's face this together, ma agra."

The half smile I mustered probably wasn't enough, but it was all I had. I climbed out of the car.

We didn't have to enter the station. The chief of police in charge of the recovery walked out before we could. He shook Cian's hand in the parking lot, looking grim and wretched.

"I'm sorry I don't have better news for you folks. We haven't found a thing, and we may never. These things happen when a body. I mean, when a person gets carried away by a rushing river. Sometimes, they turn up downstream a ways. Other times, they're carried clear to the sea. Seeing how it's been a week since the storm, I am calling off the search. I know it's hard to accept, but maybe it's time for you to return home. Think about a memorial service for your little one held where she played and had friends. I'm mighty sorry for your loss, we all are, truly, but there's no point in continuing the search at this point. Sorry." He ducked his head, turned and walked away, leaving me speechless. My knees buckled. Cian's quick action kept me from hitting the ground. This trip to Ireland had turned into a living nightmare.

"How can we consider going home without our baby girl?" My words came out a little more than a whisper.

"He's right. We may feel closer to her at home among her things and people she loved—her pony, Emilio and Rosa, Sonja and Jorge." I could hear the raw emotion in his voice.

"We should tell them in person." Yes, so all will know what a blight I am, the alien thought rang in my head.

Jewell took the news without uttering a word. My chest ached to see the anguish and grief written on her face. Death had crossed her threshold enough to make one think it'd taken up residence.

"We will keep in touch, of course. We're grateful to you for allowing us to stay on so long." Cian and I stood shoulder to shoulder in the cheery kitchen, where Jewell always seemed to be.

"Stop. It's me you were helping. I barely had it together after losing Ma and Uncle Kyle so close like that. Colleen is a joy to have around, when she's around, but work at the inn keeps her away a lot. Sure has been nice having you here." Jewell wrapped her arms about the two of us and squeezed tight.

"We'll be back if the garda finds our Erin." My words trailed off in a whisper. I broke free from the hug and went upstairs to pack, leaving Cian to reserve our flight to Antigua.

CHAPTER 13
Wish Granted

The screen door opened and slammed shut. Cora snapped her head up at the sound. She held a blue mixing bowl in her lap, snapping peas. "Well, well, look what the cat drug in. About time you showed up. I believe you have a visitor." Cora set the bowl full of peas on the table and wiped her hands on her cherry print apron, her gaze never leaving her eldest son, Liam.

My, she loved the lad, but he always seemed to be running to, or from, trouble. It looked like today it may have caught up with him. Yes, indeed.

"Me? Visitor? It's not Maeve is it, cause I told her I didn't want any more to do with her. She's been following me all over, causing trouble. Aedan showed up at the mill and popped me one in the eye thanks to her, even though I told him I didn't welcome her attentions. Look at me eye!" Liam peeled back his cap to let his mother inspect his black eye.

"Oh my stars, what's to be done with you? Get some ice on that eye right away. Your little visitor is asleep on the sofa. Let her be while you care for your eye." She raised one brow. "She's looking for her da. Her ma told her he was here. I don't suppose you be knowing anything about that, do you, mister Casanova?" She gave him a pointed look.

"Ma, I've not gotten any girl in trouble." Liam shook his head, looking confused. He turned to the fridge for ice.

"Well, it's not from your lack of opportunity. How about the Collins' niece that chased you around? She stayed with the Collins about four years ago. Never saw you out and about without her hanging on your arm. This child sorta reminds me of her. Yes, she does."

"Ma! No, I've no little ones." Shaking his head, he sat at the table to eat his lunch.

Still not convinced the child wasn't his, Cora suggested he take her out and about in order to get to know her. Maybe he could find out where, and to who, she belonged.

Cora cleared her throat to gain Liam's attention when Erin walked in, rubbing her eyes.

"Are my momma and da here?" Her furrowed gaze shifted from Cora to her son.

"No, love, she's not here. This handsome young man is going to take you out and about. Show you the sights, he will, and maybe you'll come across your ma. Anyway, Liam will make sure you have a good time. Won't you now, Liam?" She gave a pointed look toward Liam.

"Well, I suppose we could take a look around the farm and jig over to the Blarney Castle. What do ye say to that?" With a wink and a smile to Irelyn he did a jig, tossing his cap on his head and cocking it over one eye.

Giggling, Erin put her tiny hand in his. Enveloped in those long, lanky fingers, the two of them headed out the back door into the sunshine. Cora watched them from the window over the sink. A small smile played across her lips. She shook her head in consternation. The wee slip of a girl favored Liam, there was no doubt about it.

"Sheep, sheep, and more sheep, as far as your eyes can see." Liam waved his arm to encompass the surrounding countryside.

"And a donkey. I see a donkey, but it's not Gabriel." Erin frowned.

"Yes, and a donkey. That there donkey is Samson. He protects the sheep from predators. Donkeys can be mighty fierce to protect what they consider their own." Hoping to wipe the frown off Erin's face, he made a suggestion. "Do ye like to climb trees? I happen to know where the best climbing tree in all of Ireland be. If ye like, I'll take ye there."

"Oh, yes! I love to climb trees. We have mostly palm trees at home. They're no good for climbing. The native people climb them to get the coconuts, but I don't know how. They don't have branches."

"Where might home be, Erin? Where is this place the coconut trees grow?" Liam looked at her with interest.

"On the island, Antigua. Although…I guess Ireland is home too.

Da is from Ireland, and Mommy's mom and grandparents were too. I never got to meet my grandparents. They died before I lived. But I walked up the Wishing Stone backward and made a wish to meet Momma's granddad Irish, because she talks about him a whole lot. He knows all about..." Erin cupped her hand next to her mouth and whispered, "...fairies. Also, I want to meet my prince charming. Will the Druid King grant two wishes? I wished two."

"Whoa, now. That's a lot of information. Ye live in Antigua? Prince Charming, eh? You're pretty young to be thinking about Prince Charming. Plenty of time for that later. Right now we have a tree to climb. Look there." Liam pointed in front of them at a huge tree with low limbs spread out around it. He boosted Erin to the lowest branch, and up she went like a baby bear. Liam followed her up. The two of them sat across from each other, their feet dangling in the air. The sheep dotting the hills looked like clouds had dropped from the sky to rest on the green earth.

"One day I'm going to farm the land—me own land. There won't be a single sheep on it." Liam stared out over the land.

"Don't you like sheep? I like sheep, but I like my pony, Iris, better." Erin picked bark off the tree.

"A pony, ye say? What good is a pony?" Hearing Erin inhale sharply, he quickly changed the subject. "What do ye say we carve our names here in this tree where you're stripping it of its bark?"

Once they cleared an area big enough for their names on the trunk, Liam pulled a pocket knife out and carved their names.

Erin stared hard at it when he was done.

Liam jumped down out of the tree, landing on his feet. Glancing up at Erin, he saw she still stared at the tree. "Well, are ye coming down, or are ye going to sit up there till nightfall?"

"I feel funny." Erin placed a hand on her head.

"Not to worry. It's probably on account of the Blue Moon we had last night. Tends to have an effect on folks. Come on down now and we'll be off to Blarney." He held his arms out as if to catch her, so she jumped.

"Now, faeries, ye like to hear about is it? I can tell ye about the wee folk. I'll do so as we walk to Blarney, but first, let's drop back by the house to get a snack before going that way. Aye?"

"Sure, I like snacks." Erin turned her impish face up to him.

Passing through the gate to the yard, Liam followed right behind Erin.

His mother opened the back door and held it open. "Well, come on out, all of you. Step to, will you?" Her turning gaze noticed Liam and Erin. She called out, "Oh, glad I am you came back by. Your father brought a camera home! We're going to get a nice—you two hear me? Nice…" She swatted the twins, Kevin and Kyle, scooting by her out the door with a dish rag. "Picture! You're just in time." She beamed at Liam.

Jack exited the door next, toting wee Colleen, the youngest, and only, girl of the Dooley siblings.

His mother pressed a swift kiss on Colleen's head. "Bless you, Jack, for capturing this sprightly creature. All right everyone, stand against the white fence in front of the pasture. Come on, now."

Jack jostled Colleen on his hip and hopped down the steps, eliciting giggles from her. The screen door banged and Mr. Dooley joined them with the camera in one hand, grinning.

"Andy," his mother said, using his da's first name whenever she meant business. "You must be in the picture too! Ask Mr. Willy to come out to take our picture."

"Mrs. Dooley, don't be telling me what to do. I know what I'm about, so you can cease your prattling." His mother threw up her hands at da. He walked to the barn, probably to do as mom said and get the hired hand to take a picture.

In the meantime, Liam's ma watched while he and his four siblings fought for space in front of the fence. His ma usually gave them time to work things out, but after a few minutes she intervened. The final line up consisted of Liam's younger brothers, Kyle and Kevin, sitting on the fence with Liam and Jack kneeling in front of them. His ma and da stood on either side of the twins and Colleen stood in between the twin brothers. Erin stood to the side, watching.

"Darling, Erin," his ma said, "please join us. Sit in front, dear."

She settled in front and on the count of three, Mr. Willey took the photo.

"Well, now, that didn't hurt too bad, now did it?" Ma said brushing her hands together. "Don't answer that, Mr. Dooley."

Da, smart as ever, just waved and strode back to the barn with Mr. Willey. Kevin and Kyle chased Colleen around the yard, and Jack lay on his back with a piece of timothy grass sticking out of his mouth. Liam scooped up Erin and threw her on his back.

"We're off to Blarney, Ma!" He galloped toward the road with Erin. Cora waved them on their way with the dish towel.

As promised, Liam regaled Erin with tales of Druids and fairies along their journey. Erin remained quiet until he stopped to catch his breath.

"I spent my birthday here. I'm five now, you know. Momma wouldn't let me kiss the stone. Da chased me all around the Fairy Glade. I'm too fast for him, even in my princess gown."

"Slow down a wee bit, lassie, and take a breath in. Sure ye didn't kiss the stone? You're rattling on a whole lot there."

Noticing Erin no longer walked beside him, Liam turned to look back at her. "Hey now, lass, what's troubling ye?"

Erin sat in the middle of the path holding her head in her hands. "I have to feed Iris. I miss my mommy and daddy. I don't know where they are. I'm scared, and I'm never scared!" Erin sobbed.

Being the oldest of four siblings Liam witnessed plenty of tears, but Erin's anguish over her parents pricked his heart. "Now, now, sweet. Don't fret. They're probably sitting in the kitchen having a dram with Ma and Da right now waiting for us to return to the farm." Kneeling down, he ruffled her hair and wiped a tear from her cheek.

After several sniffles she nodded and stood, wiping her eyes on the fringe of her shirt. "Want me to show you where I found my favorite rock?"

The sound of Aedan's loud, male voice hailing him kicked in Liam's instincts. He stepped in front of Erin.

Aedan's red hair blazed in the sun. He strode toward Liam with his head stretched forward, his hands curled into fists by his side. He looked like an angry bull charging forward.

"Uhm, Erin, why don't ye go wait for me at the stair to the Blarney Stone." No child needed to be a witness to this kind of fury. "I'll be there shortly. Run along now. Wait there for me, and maybe I'll help ye kiss the stone."

The thought of getting to kiss the stone perked Erin up. She skipped off, leaving Liam to deal with the angry man.

Tickled by the ferns on her legs, Erin changed her pace to a run, eager to reach the steps leading up to the stone. Maybe she'd find another rock to add to her collection.

Reaching her hand into her pocket, she pulled the rock out.

The stone vibrated in her hand. She closed her fingers tight around it and continued to the steps.

The rock grew warmer the closer she came to the Blarney Stone, until it grew so hot she had to drop it upon reaching the stairs. Sitting on the bottom step, she blew on the faint red mark the rock left on her palm.

CHAPTER 14
Schemes and Strategies
Antigua 1669

Lightning split the air, followed by booming thunder. Wendy's horse, Ember, reared almost unseating her. Wendy leaned forward, wrapping her arms around the mare's neck.

Being on top of her ginger mare more than made up for her slow going and awkwardness on the ground. Her father, Mr. Kincaid, had put her on a horse before she could truly walk. Wendy became strong and capable of sitting on a horse—and Ember was not just any horse. She responded to Wendy with ease and quickness, as if she knew Wendy's thoughts and feelings before Wendy voiced or acted on them.

A palm tree fell across the path, brushing horse and rider with wet fronds. Surely, Ember rearing saved them both from being struck by the tree trunk.

Wendy stroked her hand down the side of Ember's long neck, murmuring words of praise. Once calm, she gave a tug to the left rein, guiding Ember around the fallen palm. She pushed Ember to sprint the remaining distance to the barn.

Jeremiah waited there for her. Helping her down, he held the two canes for her. He removed Ember's saddle and wiped her down with a dry rag. "Master Ethan be worried about you. He's waiting for you inside." Jeremiah nodded toward the house.

"I'm a grown woman who can take care of herself!" Wendy expelled a long sigh. "But, I do appreciate his care."

Jeremiah nodded, giving her an encouraging smile. She turned to leave the barn.

61

Outside, the storm had past as fast as it hit. Wendy entered the house by the back door into a mudroom. She lowered herself to the bench to remove her boots.

Maizie appeared from the kitchen to help her young mistress. "Shame on you, Mistress, gallivanting out in the rain. You should know better, being a grown woman."

"I couldn't have said it better myself, Maizie," Ethan said, a frown on his face. "Thank you. I'll see to Wendy now." He knelt to unlace and pull off her wet, mud-caked boots.

"Yes, Sir. I'll fix tea for the two of you." Maizie stood, giving a curt nod to Wendy.

The attitude from her servant only made her smile. "Thank you kindly, Maizie."

Wendy put her hands on either side of her husband's handsome face and leaned forward, brushing his lips with a tender kiss. "Let's have that cup of tea. I need to discuss a matter with you. I'm hoping you can help me find a resolution for."

Asking for his counsel always did the trick to lift his spirits, and today was no different. He beamed at her request.

He poured the tea Maizie brought into the parlor. The lovely aroma couldn't keep Wendy's mind from whirring about those things she told her husband she witnessed behind Ms. Calleah's home.

"Ethan, I'm frightened for them. You should've heard her! I've never seen her like that. It sent shivers down my spine."

"Darling, what can we do? It's not like we can write them a letter." He held her hand in both of his.

"Maybe I could speak to Ms. Calleah. Make her see reason." Wendy sipped her tea with her free hand, waiting on her husband's response.

"Wendy, I don't want you to seek her out." Ethan spoke slowly, with a tone demanding that she listen. "It sounds as if she's come unhinged. She may be dangerous. Besides, you have your hands full with our children. Leave things be—they'll work themselves out. I entirely doubt Ms. Calleah could have any effect on people in a future time."

Wendy held her tongue, but she had never been one to leave things be.

The next morning, Wendy jumped upon hearing the kitchen screen door creak open and shut with a bang. The familiar shuffling footsteps coming across the floor into the parlor could only belong to one person. Her arms tensed of their own accord, squeezing her youngest in her arms too tightly. He squirmed in protest with a faint fuss, threatening to grow louder. Loosening her hold, she shifted him to her shoulder and looked up into the dark eyes of Ms. Calleah. She bit her lip at the wariness she saw in them.

Wendy laid awake most of the night devising a plan that might resolve the issue. Finally, right before she drifted to sleep not too long before daybreak, she knew what must be done. Ethan would never forgive her if her plan took a bad turn. Lord, have mercy, she'd never forgive herself.

"Oh, Ms. Calleah, I can't thank you enough for coming. I'm such a mess. Everything is a mess." Wendy bounced her baby boy against her shoulder.

Her words made a smug smile pull at the corners of Ms. Calleah's mouth. Wendy forced herself not to stiffen at the woman's expression.

"I sent Maisie to fetch you as soon as this one broke his fast. I do apologize. I meant to give you respite from tending to me and mine. A nice relaxation in your mature years, but forgive me. I can't do this any longer without your help! Would you mind terribly much helping me out once again? Twould be just until this little fellow is walking and feeding himself." She paused amidst her plea to gauge Ms. Calleah's reaction. She did nothing more than cross her arms, so Wendy continued. "What do you think? It'd mean moving back into the main house. Do you mind terribly much?" Wendy stood to jostle the restless babe to her hip.

The wary look fled from Calleah's eyes. "Miss, I'd be glad to. Here, here, let me take the mite." She scooped him into her adept arms, bouncing and cooing to him in a soft, calming voice. He snuggled into her ample bosom, sucking on his fingers.

"Well, you've always had a way with children, haven't you? I'll ask Jeremiah to bring your things to your old room. Thank you, Ms. Calleah. You've set my heart at rest."

Ms. Calleah nodded and carried the baby boy up to the nursery, humming as she went.

"**S**he'd better not bring her dark magic, voodoo nonsense into this house!" Ethan's voice boomed, even though Wendy told her husband the plan was supposed to be a secret. "I'll not stand for it! Do you hear me, woman?"

She rushed out from behind the lace covered wooden partition in her night clothes. "For heaven's sake, keep your voice down. She'll hear your blustering, and I'd thank you to call me by my Christian name, if not an endearment."

"I'll not be shushed in my own house," he said though he lowered his voice anyway. Dear Ethan's bark was worse than his bite. She had to purse her lips to keep from smiling. "Am I to go about whispering all the day long?"

"I wanted to get her away from that no good brother of hers. Renewing her purpose and removing her from his evil influence could work wonders—may be just what we and she needs, for that matter. Besides, I'll be able to keep an eye on her to make sure she's not up to evil deeds."

Shaking his head, he slipped an arm under her knees and one about her back. He carried her across the room and laid her on their queen size, mahogany poster bed.

"Now, those endearments you spoke of, which do you prefer?" He placed a chaste kiss upon her forehead.

As if that would ever be enough. Wendy wrapped her arms around his neck, refusing to let him up until he kissed her properly.

Resting his forehead on hers, he looked into her eyes. "You're a demanding wench."

"That's merely one of the many things you love about—"

His deep kiss stopped her words and compelled her heart to beat faster.

In the days that followed, Wendy made sure Ms. Calleah stayed busy with the children. During the afternoons, while the little ones napped, Wendy pretended she couldn't manage to jar the guineps with the rum without the help of Ms. Calleah.

The sweet fruit tasted amazing soaked in their homegrown rum. Ethan was especially partial to the fruit prepared in this manner. He ate the concoction rolled up in his crepes, so this task especially called for Ms. Calleah's help-must keep master Ethan happy.

Wendy also could not bring in the clothes from the line, or knead the dough for their bread for the week without assistance.

Maisie didn't seem to mind the extra help, for it gave her more time to spend with Jeremiah. Thus, Ms. Calleah stayed as busy as a magpie and all went as Wendy planned—but there remained one more thing to do.

CHAPTER 15
A Picture Is Worth A Thousand Emotions
Present Day

With my suitcase zipped shut, I stood it on the hardwood floor and moved to look out the bedroom window once more. No clouds blocked the radiant sun today. The warmth emanating from the glass enveloped me, edging out the darkness residing in my being of late. Caught up in my thoughts, I didn't hear Cian until he stood beside me.

The sun shining on the grass makes the green that much more vibrant, does it not?" At my silence, he continued. "Darling, Amhuirnin, we will get through this. One day at a time." He slid his arm around my waist.

"One moment at a time is all I can handle. Cian, I must tell you something before we go home."

He squeezed my waist. "Go on, then."

So ashamed by the ignoble truth I needed to share with him, I took a deep breath first. "I've been feeling alone. Thinking terrible things about myself, and about you. Dark things."

His hold loosened on me and his head bowed. "Such as?"

"Well, things like how worthless I am as a mother, wife... hell, as a human. That you can't possibly love me, and you shouldn't. You—everyone—would be better off without me—" My voice broke. Choking back emotion, I couldn't utter another word.

His head whipped up. He grabbed me by the shoulders, whisking me around to face him. The motion caused tears to spill from my eyes. "Stop it! I love ye more than life itself. Ye are the best wife I could ever imagine. Look at me! I've seen with me own two eyes what a wonderful mother ye are. Ye couldn't be anything less, for ye love with your whole being. I don't want to hear ye talk like that ever again." The crushing hold he put on me made the breath I'd been holding whoosh out of my lungs. "Fools we are," he whispered with his mouth buried in my hair at the nape of my neck. "I thought ye blamed me."

"Cian, listen to me, please. I'm telling you now because I feel as if a dark cloud has lifted from my brain. My heart is still torn to shreds, and I meant it when I said I can only handle one moment at a time, but the dark, self-destructive thoughts have vanished. But I want you to know, in case they return and I'm not thinking clearly when we get home without our baby girl. Last night I dreamed I was standing at the cliff—the one Mira threw herself from. I stood there at the precipice with the wind whipping my hair. The ocean roiled black, slapping waves against the rock. Cian, I wanted to jump. It was so real, I tasted the salt on my lips. I'm scared, Cian."

"Together." He held me close, stroking my hair. "We'll face this life and all it hurls at us, together."

His words gave me strength for the next step that needed to be done. "What do you say we go to Erin's room and pack her things?"

Brushing tears from his eyes, he nodded and took me by the hand and led the way.

The few clothes we brought for her made for a quick job. Good thing too. It wasn't something I could bear lingering over.

Cian lifted the window seat to ensure Erin hadn't stored any of her things inside.

At seeing the sketch pad she called her picture journal, I leaned over to pick it up. "I saw her drawing in this just the other day." I flipped through the pages to find the one last drawn.

"Irelyn, look at this." Cian bent down to pick up a box. "It has your granddad's name on it." The square box he held appeared to be covered in velvet. Faded and worn, it seemed to have been well used, with Liam's name written across one corner.

Meeting Cian's gaze, I sat with him on the window seat to have a peek inside the box.

Erin's sketch pad fell open to the floor. Cian and I bumped heads in our joint effort to bend and pick it up. Seeing Erin's drawing on the page, I froze. I couldn't believe what I saw.

"Irelyn, does that look like a fairy to ye or some strange butterfly? Do ye think it's a coincidence that it's blue? Was it not a 'blue butterfly' that led ye into the wood as a lassie?"

Not able to form intelligible words, I nodded. My vision swam at the triangle-shaped drawing labeled 'Blarney' on the opposing page titled, Rocks. Gripping Cian's arm, I pointed it out to him. I closed my eyes remembering how I spelled Blarney out for her while she wrote. I assumed she drew a picture of the castle.

The drawings, simple as they were, evoked such strong memories of being sent back in time as a child. That's how I came to know Cian and his lovely parents, Brian and Ina. They took me in as one of their own until Ms. Calleah, under a Blue Moon, helped me return to my own time. To see these drawings after all these years. Drawn by my own daughter, who knew nothing of my past, could it mean…

"Irelyn, do ye think…maybe, possibly?" He didn't need to finish. The same thoughts swam in my head.

"She'd still be lost to us, but living." I whispered.

"But, she could return. You did!"

"Let's not get our hopes up. We need to think about this. What it means, if anything." I patted his arm.

Sighing, he covered my hand with his big strong one. "What do ye say we take a peek at this old box?"

"Good idea, it looks like a keepsake box."

The box contained a stack of family pictures and several letters written by granddad Irish to his ma and da. I couldn't wait to read them. They could provide a welcome distraction for Cian on the flight home, assuming Jewell didn't object to us taking them.

Thumbing through the pictures, we recognized Granddad Irish with his mother, Cora. The family pictures hanging in the hall made it possible to recognize his parents and siblings in the pictures from the box. I passed over what looked like another group picture of Granddad Irish and his siblings.

Cian cried out, startling me.

"What in blazes is wrong with you?"

"Look! Look there in the front. I can't believe it. I see it with me own eyes! It can be no other!" He grabbed the picture I'd exposed from the pile in the box and shook it in front of me.

Perturbed, I took the picture from him. My gaze grew wide, as if I could make the picture clearer if I stared hard or long enough. I couldn't utter a sound.

"She's alive. Our beautiful, wee lassie lives. The river does not have her. There can be no mistake."

"How do we get her back?" I whispered clutching the picture to my chest, as if holding her there would keep her safe from harm.

I scarce could believe it. Cross legged on the grass, in front of the family, sat a light-haired little girl. The hair, the size of her, the familiar tilt of her head all screamed Erin. Even so, she could just be a look alike—except for the shirt the girl wore. The shirt sealed it.

Before leaving Antigua, her honorary Aunt Sonja, my closest friend and former business partner, gave Erin a shirt to wear on the trip for when she missed her pony, Iris. The girl wore the same shirt in the picture. It depicted a picture of Iris with purple ribbons tied in her mane. This was our Erin, as Cian said, it could be no other. Our own Erin, in the past with her great grandfather Liam and my own granddad Irish.

"We can't leave now! She may come back. We must be here when she does."

"Yes, I think you're right." Cian squeezed my hand, but his comfort couldn't keep me from biting my lip.

"Cian, when is the next Blue Moon? That be the most likely time for her to return."

"Let's find out, I'll do an internet search." Cian pulled out his cell phone and typed in his question. "Curse it all! There's not to be another for thirteen months."

"More than a year away? Oh, Cian, our baby girl will be nearly seven years old by then. I can't bear the thought. How can we stay here that long? Dare we return to Antigua?" I let my head drop into my hands, overwhelmed by the various implications.

His strong, steady hands clasped my wrists and pulled me up. With the tip of his nose to mine, he looked unblinking a me. "Irelyn, our wee lassie is alive. Even if we have to wait six years before we get her back, at least we get her back. Even if she never returns to her own time, at least we know she didn't drown. She's with family. She'll be well cared for." His half smile turned into a gentle kiss to my mouth.

"You're right, as usual. It's a blessing, not an easy one, mind you, but a blessing all the same."

Doing my best to return a faint smile, I suggested we discuss what to tell Jewell when she returned home from her errands.

The two of us spent the better part of an hour going back and forth on whether or not to tell Emilio and Rosa and Sonja and Jorge about our missing Erin. But there remained no other way to explain our continued absence. The difficult phone call had to be made.

"Remember they don't know about our history with time travel," I said. "So just say we are confident she'll be found and we're going to stay until she's returned to us."

"When I get one of them on the phone? Why do I have to be the one to call? I think ye should do it."

"I don't think I can, Cian. How about we do it together on speaker? Just make sure they understand we don't need them to join us. We will tell them she'll be found before they could even get here." I rested my head on his shoulder.

"Allright, we'll do it together. But since ye are the one with all the thoughts of what to say, I expect ye to do a lot of the saying."

As for Jewell, we agreed not to show her the picture, and only to tell her we had a change of heart about leaving.

"Well, bless you both. I'm glad, I am, you'll be staying. And don't be thinking you have to help me with the sheep. A blessing it was, for sure, while Ma and Uncle Kyle were ill and after. But I've ran this farm for many years without the two of you, and I suspect I can keep at it." Jewell propped both her feet on the coffee table and sunk back into the couch.

Rising from the green chenille ribbed chair, I crossed the room to plant a kiss on her forehead. "Thank you, Jewell. We're just not ready to give up on Erin yet."

"I can't rightly blame you. You're welcome to stay as long as you like. The two of you are family, and I most enjoy the company." She rested her head on the back of the couch with her eyes closed, a smile playing at her lips.

"I'm going up to join Cian for a nap. I'll cook dinner tonight when I get up in about an hour. It's high time I returned to the living."

71

Chapter 16
Silly Girls and Bully Boys
Cork, 1952

Bent over at the waist, Erin held her hair back at the base of her neck, walking in circles.

"Hello, there. What are you doing, are you crippled or hurt?"

She turned her face to see who spoke. A boy, blocking the sun, caused an unearthly glow around him. Sunrays burst from his shining hair, calling to mind the stories Grammy told her from the Old Testament. "Are you an angel?"

"Do I look like an immortal being? You must be daft!" The young boy stood with his feet planted and hands on his hips, frowning down at her.

"No, you don't." Straightening up, Erin stood tall and lifted her chin. "You don't act like one either. Angels aren't rude! Go away before you step on my rock. I dropped it."

"So. The only thing rocks are good for are slingshots. You seem too prissy to use a slingshot."

Too prissy? Well she'd show him. Erin stepped toward him with fists clenched at her side.

Holding up his hands, he took a step back. "I'm going. I've got better things to do than stand here talking to some silly little girl. I'm headed to ask the Druid King for a wish." He nodded his head in the direction of the Wishing Steps. "You've gotta be brave and strong to get a wish." The sideways glance he gave her said he never thought she would be either of those things.

"Then you might as well stay here and help me find my rock.

73

Besides, I got a wish from the Druid King already. It was easy."

"Shut up! How old are you?" He stared wide eyed at her.

"I did!" Erin stomped her foot. "I'm five. How old are you?"

"I'm eight, that's why I'm so much smarter than you.

But you can come watch me get my wish. I bet you didn't even do it right." He crossed his arms, acting all superior.

"Did too!" She stuck her tongue out at the boy and turned to look for Liam. He still stood toe-to-toe with the red faced man. She waved to him but he was too engrossed in his loud conversation to notice her. So, she followed the rude boy, forgetting about her special rock.

Sitting on a rock, Erin watched the sandy-haired boy walk down the steps. Knowing better than to ask him his wish, she asked, "Why do you want a wish, anyway?"

"I'm an orphan and I've run away. I won't go back to the home, so I'm asking for a wish."

"Oh." Not feeling so angry towards him now, she gasped at his stumbled on the way back up the steps backward. "Keep your eyes closed! You're almost to the top!"

"Shush, will ya?" Once he reached the top, he jumped in the air with his fists raised high above his head.

His exuberance made Erin laugh.

He ran over and plopped down on the rock beside her like a victor. "Whew! Now to wait for my wish. Aren't you kinda too young to be out here by yourself? Are you an orphan too?"

Right now it felt like she was. Instant tears welled in her eyes. "I can't find ma and da, or cousin Jewell, not even Gabriel the donkey. He doesn't like me!" She dissolved in a heap of sobbing.

"They're probably looking for you right now." The awkward pat he did on her shoulder wasn't helping. "Maybe if we're quiet we'll hear them calling. Ssh now, listen." His gaze snapped over her head toward the trees. He put his arm around her shoulders. "Do you believe in fairies? Hang it, I think I just saw one."

She turned her head to see what he looked at, the air shimmering around her.

CHAPTER 17
Hope
Cork, Present Day

Cian's show of stiff control ended the moment he set the phone down. He shook his head. "Never pleasant to ruin someone's day, but they needed to know. I'm glad the telling is over with."

"Me too." I would have given anything to spare Sonja, Emilio, and Rosa those phone calls, but leaving them in the dark about the situation wasn't right. "They were very quiet. Think they're okay?"

"Aye, they're sure to be in shock. They love our lassie so."

"I'm hoping we convinced them to stay put." I laid my arm across my forehead and leaned back in the chair.

"I'm thinking we could use some cheering up. Come on, come with me. Up ye go." Pulled by my hands, Cian led me to the kitchen door, winking at Jewell on his way past her.

"The day is young." Jewell smiled and continued rolling out dough for the biscuits we'd eat over the next couple of mornings. "See that the two of you enjoy it. Why don't you visit the old estate on the coast? It's a castle, really, called Bell Manor for the bell that hangs in one of the towers. It used to be a real beauty with fantastic gardens and fountains back in its day. The locals say they hosted the best fox hunt in the country at one time. There was an enormous barn for the horses. Real fancy, it was for a horse. People sent their children there for riding instruction. It's fairly dilapidated now, but as you walk around it's easy to see its former glory. Really, pretty amazing."

An old abandoned castle peaked my interest. "What happened to it? Why is it dilapidated now?"

"Well, the original Lord of the manor lost his wife in childbirth. Crazy with grief, he sent the midwife away with the babe. The Lord became a drunken recluse, refusing visitors. The staff eventually all left after suffering his verbal abuse. A sad tale, really. But the grounds and manor are worth a see."

"That is a sad tale. I'd like to see it sometime, but Cian has somewhere he's taking me right now."

"Aye, we have high plans." The way he raised his eyebrows made me wonder what 'high' had to do with our destination. "I wonder what became of the wee babe. We're off to enjoy the sunshine." He offered Jewell another wink and pushed me out the door. He guided me past the barn and even out through the yard's gate.

"Where are you taking me?"

"We're going to climb a tree."

I hadn't climbed a tree since the age of twelve. Mother asked me to help her pick the ripe fruit off the pear tree in the orchard beyond the backyard. A tree planted by Granddad Irish and my father after mom and dad moved into the house.

Climbing into the lower branches, I dropped the pears down to mom, who put them in her bushel basket. The higher fruit I couldn't reach without climbing farther up the tree. Cautioned by my mother, up I went.

On my tippy toes I stretched my arm out as far as I could reach and plucked the last pear to toss down to her. Proud of myself, I danced a jig on the branch to make her laugh. My foot slipped and I landed at her feet on my side. My mom had always blamed herself for my broken arm, but the fault really belonged to me.

I came out of my memories to find Cian leading me across the main pasture dotted with sheep. We weren't enough of a bother for them to stop their placid munching on the grass, along the fence, close to the river.

Even though, I now knew the river didn't take Erin, chills still struck my body at the sight of it. Today, the water gurgled over and around the rocks and tree roots in no particular hurry. It didn't appear to be dangerous and capable of sweeping anyone, or thing, away. However, given the right circumstances, I'd seen the river swelled past its banks, sweeping everything in its path along with it, trees, sheep, and even people. Rivers were not respecters of persons.

"Here we are, love." Cian stood under an oak tree with low sprawling branches. Hefting himself up onto the lowest one, he reached a hand down to me. I held onto his arm and walked my feet up the tree trunk till I could twist my body onto the branch next to him.

"Here we are," I said with a grin, repeating his words back to him.

He angled his head at the tree trunk. I followed his gaze. About a foot above the branch we perched on someone had carved Liam & Erin, August 1959 in the tree.

The sight of Erin's name with granddad Irish's made my eyes swim. "It's her, isn't it. It's our Erin."

Granddad Irish had died before I went to Antigua and found Cian. It always bothered me Granddad Irish and Erin hadn't known each other. Smiling, I rubbed my hand over their names in the smooth wood.

The two of us sat in silence. Something about this spot brought a strong sensation of closeness to Erin, as well as granddad. I would have been content to sit on the branch leaning against Cian, who leaned against the tree trunk all day.

His sudden hop to the ground surprised me. Opening up his backpack, he pulled one of Jewell's quilts out and spread it on the tall grass in the shade of the tree. With his lifted hands he helped me slide down facing him. My gratitude for the man I married grew even more. Here under the tree my heart found peace, in the same spot Erin and Granddad had both once occupied. The tree being another physical reminder our Erin lived.

Cian reached into his shirt and pulled out granddad's letters to his ma. "I thought it'd be a good time and place to read them." He looked at me with eyebrows raised, as if seeking my approval.

"Yes, of course. Maybe he says something of Erin."

CHAPTER 18
The Letters

"Here goes." Cian held the first letter in his hand and began to read...

Dear Ma,

I've arrived safely in America. Sorry, I am it took so long to write, seeing how I promised I would as soon as I disembarked. But Ma, I've so much to tell ye. Really big news! I think you'll be pleased to hear.

First, give Da me apologies for making such a ruckus about being sent to America. Honestly, it wasn't that I didn't want to come here. I do love me an adventure. I was more offended about the why. I swear to ye, Ma, that wee girl, Erin, did not belong to me and I didn't have anything to do with her disappearance. How could Da think such a thing of me? I searched everywhere for her. Anyway, I've no wish to rehash any of that. But, if you hear anything of her, let me know would ya?

New York is crowded, dirty, and noisy, but Ma, the energy—It fairly vibrates with it. The twins would love it.

I got a job on a farm. We're moving to Virginia. That's right, I said we. I got married, Ma! We met on the ship. The Captain married us. I know it was quick, but we're good for each other and I love her, Ma. She be a good Irish lass. Now ye understand why it took me so long to write. Her name is Oleta. Is it not the prettiest name ye ever heard?

All for now,
Your ever-loving son,

Liam

"It seems our wee lassie caused a stir being in the past."
"Apparently, so. Read the next one."

Dearest Ma,
Oleta thanks ye for the package. She said it's the finest shawl she's ever worn. Tell Da I'm almost ready to buy me own farm land. They don't much like sheep here, cattle is preferred. Not that I'm concerned about that since I plan to farm, not ranch.
Any of the family is welcome to come over for a visit. Missing all of you.

Your ever-loving son,

Liam

"Short one. He sounds homesick. Poor Granddad Irish. Keep Reading."
"There be just one more."

Da,
For once in my life, I have no words. I guess ye received my telegraph? I imagine yer having a hard time without Ma by yer side. Please know it hurts me not to have been able to come. Our baby was due any day and it had been a difficult pregnancy. I couldn't leave Oleta and she definitely couldn't travel. I feel sure Ma can

look down and see our beautiful baby girl, Meghan.
If it'd help, feel free to send any of the kids to us, if they
need work. Take care of yourself.

Your son,

Liam

"That's so sad. Doesn't sound like he had a very good relationship
with his father." I laid on my back next to Cian looking into the tree,
hoping my sweet Erin wasn't the reason for the rift between father and
son.

CHAPTER 19
Coming Home

Lying on the quilt together, fingers entwined, I gazed up into the rustling leaves in the breeze. The dappled sun warmed my skin. The soothing location, combined with the myriad of emotions I grappled with since discovering Erin lived, but in another time, took their toll on me. I drifted to sleep.

I heard Erin's voice as if from a great distance. Squeezing Cian's hand, I remained still. I kept my eyes closed, wanting the dream to continue. I did my best to mute out Cian's light snores beside me.

Again, Erin called out, closer this time. Chills chased over my skin. My eyes flew open wide. I scrambled to my knees, trying to look in every direction at once.

"What's wrong? What is it?" Cian sat up rubbing a hand through his thick, wavy hair.

The breath I didn't realize I held whooshed out when I saw him tense. He heard it too! We both couldn't be dreaming.

"Ma! Da! Over here!" I couldn't believe my eyes. Erin ran toward us, across the field. Her glorious strawberry-blonde hair, shining in the sun, flew behind her. I never saw a prettier sight, but she wasn't alone. A young boy ran behind her. Cian and I both jumped to our feet. I didn't care if I dreamed it or not, it felt like heaven.

But Erin didn't fade away, she kept running toward us, waving both hands in the air.

Cian and I closed the distance. He swept her up into his arms. Sobbing, I ran my hands over her hair and face.

"Don't cry, Momma. I'm sorry, I got lost in the storm."

"Lassie, it's all right. It's not your fault. Ye hear?"

"Da is right. Nothing is your fault. These are happy tears." Taking a few deep cleansing breaths, I gestured to the quiet boy watching our reunion.

Erin wriggled out of her da's arms and stood beside the boy who stood at least a foot taller than her. "This is...what's your name?" She frowned at him.

She didn't know the boy's name? I shared a look with Cian. We both turned again to the dark-haired boy standing beside our wee lassie.

Maybe my raised eyebrows looked too threatening. He remained silent, staring back at us until Erin elbowed him in the side.

"Ian is my name. I don't feel so well. I might—" He turned his back to us and threw up.

Such an unexpected action jarred me into motion. "Oh! You poor thing. Come, lie down." I led him to our blanket, all the time keeping my eyes on Erin. I didn't plan to let her out of my sight until we got her back home to Antigua—maybe not even then.

"My head hurts," Erin said reaching the blanket. "Can I lay down too?"

Before either of us could reply, she laid across one corner of the blanket. They both were asleep as soon as their heads touched down. I'd never seen anything like it. I stared at Cian, with the only sound being the wind rustling through the leaves above.

I had too many questions to remain silent for long. "The moon?"

Cian shook his head. "No. No Blue Moon."

Looking at the two sleeping children, I couldn't resist lying down next to Erin to gather her in my arms. Cian sat cross legged on the blanket with a grin on his face. A permanent crease had developed between his eyebrows these past few weeks. Even though it didn't detract from his rugged good looks, it did my heart good to see a real grin on the man's face.

The sun sat a little lower in the sky, yet the children continued to sleep. Standing up, I stretched out stiff muscles, bending side to side, then forward and backward.

With only one eye cracked open, Cian watched me.

"When I traveled to your time and you found me unconscious, close to the creek, how long did I sleep?"

"Ye? Mean when ye tripped me and made me spill me mushrooms? Well now, ye were a slip of a lassie. Looked more like a ghost, ye did. Me self, I thought you'd never wake. No telling how long ye slept before ye tripped me. Da carried ye home and ye slept till late the next morning."

"I woke on my own the next morning?"

"Aye, and me heart's never been the same." He winked at me, and my heart skipped a beat.

His stomach grumbled loud enough for me to hear. "What do ye say we carry these two to the house? If they sleep through the journey they can finish their sleep in a comfy bed while we fix a bite to eat."

"I call the smallest one." I bent over and lifted Erin up. Her head laid on my shoulder with her legs around my waist.

Cian slid his arms under the slight boy and scooped him up with Jewell's quilt.

By the time we reached the house we both were breathing heavy. The weight of my load left me no choice but to pause for a moment to catch my breath. Cian followed on my heels up the stairs. He placed the boy in the room Erin stayed in and I laid her in our bed.

I stopped at the door for one last look before going downstairs, sliding my arms around my handsome husband. "Thank-you for getting me through this. You're my rock."

"Oh, aye? Are ye saying I'm hard headed?" He bent his head down, resting his forehead on mine.

"No doubt, you are hard headed, but that's not what I was referring to." I angled my head just enough so our lips touched.

Cian crushed his mouth to mine, pinning me to the door jamb with his hard body. Weeks of pent up emotion released in a single kiss. My knees gave out. He held me up by my elbows, slowing the kiss. I still clung to him.

Placing a soft kiss on my forehead, he said, "Ye are me own rock, too."

A note left by Jewell said she had gone to the Blarney Castle Inn to have dinner with Colleen. I helped Cian scour the refrigerator for food that could be cooked up quickly. Deciding on omelets, Cian got busy whisking eggs and I diced the ham. The simple meal we devoured in no time.

"What should we tell Jewell?" I said at the kitchen table, pushing my empty plate away.

"We tell her the truth. We were resting under the tree when Erin and this young lad came from across the field." He stood up and took our plates to the sink.

"Leaving out where she's been?" I said. "We let her draw her own conclusions?"

"I think it's best, but we can play it by ear." He pulled his phone from his pocket. "I think we have a couple long distance phone calls to make."

Grinning, I leaned with my arms on the table. He sat back down with the phone and handed it to me.

Gingerly holding the stem to avoid the thorns, Rosa snipped dead flowers off. Purge the bad to make way for new growth, she thought to herself. If it were only as easy to take these trimmers and snip out the bad thoughts crowding my brain. My poor baby girl lost and alone. She has to be alive. She just has to— "OUCH!"

Startled by her ringing phone, a sharp thorn snagged her skin. Rosa shook her hand and dug out the phone from her apron pocket with the other one. She sucked her pricked finger before answering. "Hello?" she said, her tone a little too short for a polite greeting.

"Rosa? Is something wrong?"

"Oh, dear me, no. Sorry, Irelyn. I'm pruning the roses while Emilio walks Iris. We try to come over every day for the pony." Rosa walked over to the porch steps and sat down under the shade of the roof where she could enjoy the Caribbean breeze. "How are you and Cian holding up?"

"Well, that's why I'm calling. Cian and I were resting in the pasture on a quilt when Erin and a young boy came running across the grass like sunshine bursting through the clouds."

"What? Oh, my stars! Is she okay? Is she hurt? Where has she been? Who is this boy? Oh my, I can't believe it. It's too good. It's—"

"Rosa, Rosa, I know. Yes, it's an answered prayer. She seems fine. She's sleeping right now. They both are. We don't know much yet. We're letting them sleep. We wanted you and Emilio to know right away that she's okay. Our baby girl is alive and well. I'll let you go now so you can tell Emilio, and please do tell Sonja and Jorge too, would you?"

"Yes, yes, of course. Bless you. Come home quickly." Saying their goodbyes, they each clicked off. Rosa gathered her skirt and ran to the corral to relay the good news to Emilio.

CHAPTER 20
That's Life
Cork, Present Day

"**B**e careful!" I covered my eyes, sure Ian and Erin's spin in the mud puddle would tip the four by four over. Erin clutched Ian's shirt, laughing and screaming in delight.

Cian came running from the barn in time to get splattered with mud. Jewell and I laughed from the safety of the porch steps.

"Ye think it's funny, do ye?" Cian said with a glint in his eye. A telltale look of danger. I stood and backed up the steps, turning my back on him wouldn't be wise.

"Well, you must admit it's your turn to be covered in mud." I took my turn during the storm the night Erin went missing.

Cian bent and scooped up a handful of mud. I reached for the screen door. Ian watched wide eyed.

"Do it, Daddy!" Erin said, egging her father on.

"Now hold on a wee minute, Cian." Jewell put her hands out.

As if on cue, the phone rang in the kitchen. All five of us scrambled indoors.

The last several weeks had been spent working with the Adoption Authority of Ireland. Jewell had taken to Ian and he to her. He craved attention and she gave him plenty, as well as home cooked meals and a purpose.

Ian's chores started soon after breakfast, helping with the sheep. He acted like it was the most important job in the world. He fairly shone with pride.

Cian and I had thought to take him back to Antigua with us, until we witnessed the bond forming between him and Jewell. Even young Colleen took a liking to him. She taught him and Erin how to play Go Fish with cards.

Above the age of seven, Ian had a say about whether or not he wanted to be adopted. This presented no problem. The problem came when no record of his birth, or even his existence could be found.

Jewell answered the phone and put it on speaker so we all could hear.

"Since the young man insists he wasn't abandoned by his family during a visit from another country, but that he ran away from the orphanage…"

"It's true! That's what I done. I've never been outta this country," Ian said.

"Now son, the orphanage swore they've never seen you or the likes of you, but, historically speaking, the orphanages in these here parts don't have an exactly squeaky clean reputation. They're even known for selling the kiddos to Americans in the fifties and sixties." My heart warmed to see Jewell cover Ian's ears to protect him from these hard facts. "Now, I asked my Guarda to distribute a bulletin with Ian's picture across Ireland. They did so, but they're used to dealing with missing children, not found ones." I looked at Jewell, wondering where this conversation would lead. "Since this last-ditch effort didn't turn up any information, Jewell, you're to be allowed to adopt the young man—assuming you still wish to. He's not been giving you any trouble now has he?"

"Jewell, answer him, will ye?" Cian shook her arm. I thought she looked dazed.

"What did you say?" She pressed her palm to her cheek. "He's mine?"

"Yes, ma'am. That's what I'm saying. You will need to fill out the necessary paperwork about Ian, so they can create a permanent record for him so he can attend school and such."

"Yes, yes, of course." Her eyes glistened. "I've gained a son." I took the phone away from her after she rang off.

Thrilled by the news, Cian, Erin, Ian, and I held hands and danced around Jewel. She held her hands to her face, laughing.

Jewell shushed us once again to call the Blarney Inn to tell her daughter, Colleen, the good news about Ian.

"Colleen suggested we have a party to welcome Ian officially to the family. She offered to use her connections at the Inn to reserve a section of the dining room. Won't that be fun?" Jewell said.

"Yes!" Cian and I both replied in unison. I laughed when Ian raised his arm in the air and did a fist pump.

We went from mourning to throwing a party in a matter of minutes. That's life, as my father used to start singing when, as a child, I'd cry or complain about something. He'd burst out singing, "That's life, and as funny as it may seem, some people get their kicks by stomping on a dream. But I don't let it get me down, cuz this fine old world keeps spinning around," by Frank Sinatra. He would pick me up and spin me around. I always ended up laughing. I sure do miss him, and Mom too.

The following day, Cian said, "Since we're leaving Ireland soon, why don't we go explore Bell Manor as Jewell suggested."

Having forgotten all about the dilapidated castle, I enthusiastically agreed. Jewell declined to accompany us, saying she had too much to do to get ready for the party. So, Cian, Erin, Ian, and I piled into the rental car for a little road trip.

The sun shone. Cool breezes blew through the rolled down windows. The kids had their hands stuck out the back ones. Carefree, we drove the long winding road to the coastal manor.

A change came over Ian the closer we got to the manor. He stared out the window, when only moments earlier he had laughed and carried on along with Erin.

Cian stopped in the circle drive in front of the main house. Stepping out of the car, I turned to admonish Erin and Ian to remain with us the whole time.

"Ian, aren't you going to get out of the car?"

"Come on, Ian. Let's go! I want to see the fancy barn." Erin's urgent little voice would not be denied much longer.

"I'm coming. Hold your horses, will ya?"

"Lad, ye might as well get used to being hurried by a woman now. It'll make it easier for you as a young man." Cian blew me a kiss. His action didn't save him from a scowl from me.

Erin skipped and twirled around everywhere we went, thrilled to be at another castle. "Mommy, I wish I had my princess gown, or at least my tiara. Can we get a crown for Ian?"

This drew Ian out of his trance. "What? I'm not wearing no crown. No way. You're daft."

"No need for the insults, Lad," Cian siad, chiding him. "The lassie wishing ye to have a crown is a compliment to ye. She means yer worthy of one."

"Sorry." Ian kicked the dirt. "I wouldn't like to wear one."

"Now, that's an acceptable reply. It's okay, Ian. Erin, let's go see the fancy barn." Cian's suggestion was all it took to restore the former good cheer.

The barn stood two stories tall. Once upon a time the second floor would have stored hay. The room off the main stall area must have once held the tack. I could imagine all the fine saddles that once hung there on the cedar walls. The stall doors had iron bars with a cursive B in the middle. Buckets still hung in each stall for the horses long since gone. Their names, however, were still carved with elaborate lettering in wood over each stall.

"Oh, Da, Iris would love her name on her stall."

"Oh, aye? We'll see what we can do for her."

Ian walked the length of the barn, reading each name. I watched him, curious at what had brought on his somber mood.

Next, we hunted for the fountain. Finally, we found it hidden under an enormous Weeping Willow. Even-though, water didn't run through and over it, gurgling on its cheerful way, I could see it how it once would've been.

A beautiful mermaid, carved from white marble, rested on her curved tail, with both hands extended up holding a seashell. The water would've come through the shell to fall down into the pool adorned with seahorses, fish, and other carved shells.

I'd never seen anything so beautiful. I mourned for the beauty of the estate now hidden and wasting away. Such a shame.

"Well, we have a party to get ready for. We'd better get back!"

Cian gave a whistle when Erin and I came down the stairs in our new party dresses. She did a spin, so I followed suit.

"Finest two lasses me eyes have ever seen, I do believe. Hold up, here comes another one." Jewell entered the kitchen wearing a full-length dress and her hair swept up in a knot. I thought she looked regal.

A scrubbed clean, hair slicked back, dressed up Ian walked in.

"Who are ye and where is Ian? Ye know, the young, scruffy lad?" Cian said. I elbowed him in the side. Ian looked so handsome I didn't want him to feel self-conscious on his special night.

Ian frowned. "Ah, do I have to wear this noose?" He pulled at his tie.

"Leave it be. You're such a handsome young man," Jewell said. I noticed Erin didn't have anything to say.

The balloons and streamers hanging from the ceiling of the party room lit up both Erin's and Ian's eyes.

"Be sure to tell Colleen you like her decorations." I said.

They nodded and ran off in the direction of the cake Jewell made. My stomach reminded me it had been too many hours since I'd last eaten.

"What do you say we go see how the food turned out the chef prepared?"

"As ye say." Cian took me by the hand and led me across the room to the buffet where we met up with Colleen.

After a brief hug, she said, "I'm so glad you suggested the troupe that played here during your first visit. When I rang them up and told them about the party, and why we're throwing it, they said they'd work it into their schedule. Turns out the violinist lived at the orphanage himself when he was a tot."

"How sweet. That's perfect. I can't wait to see them. Oh, look, here they are now."

The two musicians needed little time to tune their instruments. Once they began playing a lively tune, a guy and a girl danced the traditional Irish steps with flicks and kicks.

"There's me Irish lassie." I followed Cian's gaze to see Erin on the small dance floor raising her knees with toes pointed, dancing a jig.

"Granddad Irish would be so proud. I wish he could see her."

"How do ye know he's not watching, dancing his own jig right now?" Cian put an arm around my shoulders. I shrugged in response.

"Cian, look at Ian! He's dancing those steps like he's done it his

93

whole life. Do you think they had lessons at the orphanage back then?"

"I doubt it. Makes ye wonder does it not?"

"Makes you wonder about what?" Jewell said. She ate from a plate of food in her hand.

How would he dig himself out of this one? I quirked an eyebrow at Cian.

"Where yer newly acquired lad learned to dance like that."

"He's a natural I reckon," Jewell said.

"The party is a great success, Jewell. It was so sweet to see how overwhelmed Ian became opening presents from all the neighbors and friends of Colleen's. Laughter, music, and dancing is exactly what I needed after all the stress of Erin missing."

"Yes, yes indeed."

By the end of the following week, Cian, Erin, and I finally headed home to Antigua. Cian and I were beyond thankful to be returning with Erin in tow.

Inside the baggage claim area at the airport, we were greeted with cheers, whoops, and hollering. Emilio, Rosa, Sonja, and Jorge all stood waving to us. Embarrassed by so much noise, my first inclination wanted to pretend I didn't know them, but I hadn't seen them in so long, I just couldn't. I ran and embraced each of them instead.

"Don't cry Nanny. I'm okay," Erin said. I patted Rosa's back as she held Erin.

"Give her aunty a turn, will ya?" Sonja said. I took Erin from Rosa and guided her to a weeping Sonja. After many hugs we made it out of the airport with our luggage.

Later in the evening, after supper, Cian and I rang Jewell to let her know we were safely home.

"So glad you called. I'm lying in bed researching curriculum for Ian. I'm thinking I'll homeschool him for a year to bring him up to par. He's so intelligent, yet there's so much he acts like he's never seen or heard of before. If I leaned toward superstitions or fancies, I'd think he's been living with the faeries or from another time. It's so peculiar."

"Ha, well, now tis a good thing we know ye to be a sensible one." Cian winked at me.

"Yes, I think homeschooling sounds like a good idea for a while,

Jewell."

Though she left the call pleased, part of me wished I'd told her the truth, but even I didn't know the whole story yet. "Now we have her home safe and sound and surrounded by everything and everyone she loves. I think it's a good time to ask her how she spent the time while she was lost."

"Let's go put our wee lassie to bed and have a wee chat with her."

Walking into her room on the floor beneath ours, I had to smile. Our daughter lay across her rug with a purple pony sporting a pink mane. Just a short while ago, I thought to never see her sprawled across this rug again. I would've been happy to stand here and watch her forever. Was it normal to not want your child to grow up? Had my own mother felt this way?

"What are you drawing, Sweetheart?"

"My friend, Liam. He was a lot of fun, and he knows about fairies."

My heart skipped a beat hearing her so casually talk about meeting her great grandfather as a young man. Except, of course, she didn't realize that's who she spent time with.

Cian walked past me and sat on her bed. "Come on up here, Princess, and I'll tuck ye in."

"Are you going to read me a story?" she said putting her colored pencils back in the box.

"Yer ma and I were hoping ye'd tell us about what all ye did when ye were lost."

Her lips stuck out in a frown. "Will you get mad at me?"

"No, darling. We only are curious about who you spent your time with, and what you did. That's all." I sat on the bed opposite of Cian.

She climbed on the bed and let her da tuck the covers around her. Her lips spread into a broad smile. "I met a donkey that wasn't Gabriel."

"Oh, aye? Did he tell ye his name?"

Erin giggled at her father's words. "No, but Liam called him Samson." A sad look came over our precious child's face and she said, "Miss Cora had to make my feet better. They hurt-she put medicine on them."

"Oh honey, I'm sorry you hurt your feet. I hope you told Cora thank you."

"Of course she did, and she was a brave lassie too." My strong husband spoke with such love and pride in his voice it nearly made me teary.

Erin nodded and continued. "Liam took me to Blarney Castle but he argued with an angry man. And Ian saw a fairy after he almost fell on the Wishing Steps."

Cian and I looked at each other. "Anything else happen, darling?"

"Hmmm. Oh! I lost my favorite rock. It got hot, hot, hot in my hand till I dropped it. I looked for it, but Ian came and I helped him. Then we were in the field. I didn't find my rock, Momma." She pouted.

"That's okay, darling. You drew a picture of it, and maybe that is where your rock belongs." I brushed my hand down her hair.

"Is that by chance where ye found the rock to begin with?"

"Yes, on my birthday trip." She closed her eyes.

Cian and I kissed her and left her to sleep.

Walking back up stairs to our own room, my mind swirled around the rock she mentioned. "That answers some questions. Could she have picked up granddad Irish's rock that I returned? What's the likeliness of that?"

"Stranger things have happened, Lass."

Yes, indeed, especially for someone like me who had experienced time travel. Sitting on the side of the bed, I stared at the floor.

Erin's words played over and over in my head. I longed to ask her so many questions about Granddad Irish. Did he seem happy? Could she see the sparkle in his eye and spring in his step? Did he make her feel like the most important little girl in the world? How about fairies—did he tell her tales of fairies?

"Irelyn?" Cian said, interrupting my maudlin thoughts. "Are ye feeling all right?" He sat beside me and placed a hand on my back.

For his concerned expression I offered him my best soft smile. "Yes. I'm fine, just feeling a little emotional hearing Erin talk about granddad Irish like he's the boy next door, or a big brother. It's so surreal. I've wished she could've known him, but I can't very well tell her she met her dead great grandfather, now can I? I miss him so much, Cian."

"I know ye do, Lass." He pulled me under his arm until my head rested on his shoulder. "A fine man, your grandda. He loved ye so, and now we understand he loved our lassie too." Cian always said the right thing to make me feel better.

CHAPTER 21
A Snake in the Grass
Antigua 1669

"I s that all I need do, Mr. Winthrop?" Wendy lay the quill down and blew on her signature.

"Yes, yes, those papers will take care of everything as you specified. Can't say I understand your intent. However, you are of sound mind and body, and it's your land to do with as you please. I have seen stranger requests, so rest assured, your wishes will stand." He stacked the papers and placed them in the vault.

"It's simple, really, Mr. Winthrop. I wish the land to remain in my family until there are no more Kincaid's or Whitaker's to inherit. Then, I wish no one to have it except a Cian Gallagher or his descendants. Some of the property may be sold should circumstances dictate the necessity, but at least five acres must remain. The remaining acreage may only be sold to Cian Gallagher or his descendants. None other. Are we clear?"

"Yes, yes. That's what the papers state." The solicitor came out from behind his desk to clasp her hand. "Tell Ethan hello for me. He best be on the lookout for trouble from the French. Rumors are growing the Frenchies mean to leave St. Kitts to invade other islands. They'll steal away the slaves at the very least, if not destroy the sugar mills."

"I'll relay the news. Have no doubt, my husband and Jeremiah will keep a watch over the sea." Nodding him a curt good day, she left.

Wendy pulled her wide brimmed hat low over her eyes and stepped out into the sun. Jeremiah jumped down at her appearance and helped her into the buggy.

She loved riding in the open buggy, basking in the warm sun and cool island breezes. She inhaled the sweet scent of the flowers native to the island. Oleander, Hibiscus and Plumeria were her favorites.

Looking out over the sea, she shivered at the idea of French ships in the waters. She shook her head to rid herself of the farfetched imaginings. She had more pressing problems.

Ms. Calleah's brother had become an annoyance of late. He'd come to the house on two occasions she knew of, pestering Ms. Calleah. She truly didn't want him around the children. She needed to speak to her about the problem. Ms. Calleah wouldn't allow any harm to befall the children, but still.

Humming, Ms. Calleah dropped blackberries into her wooden bucket. She eyeballed the grass before stepping to the next bush.

"Snakes do love the berries," She said, giving those critters even more warning than just her humming to slither away. Her leather boots gave her some protection too.

"Ol' Mr. Kincaid had them made for her. There'll never be another like him. No sirree." Speaking her thoughts didn't hurt nothing either. "I'm gonna make a blackberry pie for after supper. Wendy does love a blackberry pie—always has. It was Ol' Mister Kincaid's favorite too— bless him. But don't you worry, snakes, there'll be plenty berries left for you, so you just be leaving me alone."

The hairs on the nape of her neck raised up. She whirled around, coming face to face with Cal. "What you mean by scaring me so?" She turned back to the berry bush.

"You seem to have forgotten about helping me."

"Psh! You be a grown man. What help of mine do you need?" She glanced over her shoulder. His sulky, menacing face annoyed her. "And, by the way, don't come to the big house no more. You ain't got no business there any longer."

"I'll come and go as I please, Sister. Besides, you're supposed to help me take vengeance on Irelyn. Or did you forget what she's done to me?"

"I haven't forgotten. I just wonder if maybe you deserved it."

"Why, I…"

Ms. Calleah whipped around to see his fist raised to her. She glared at her younger brother with a look meant to remind him she was an

Obeah. "I am not your vessel to do your bidding. If you want revenge, then seek it yourself, under tonight's blue moon, but remember, 'vengeance is mine,' says the Lord. You seek revenge at you own peril. Now, get out of my sight!"

Spitting at the ground in front of her feet, he spun on his heel and stalked off.

"Not all snakes slither," she said to herself. She expelled a long breath and finished berry picking.

Snapping the green beans in half, Wendy dropped them in the bowl she held in her lap. Maizie sat next to her doing the same. Nearby, Ms. Calleah washed the children's clothes in a whiskey barrel, agitating them with a stick—much like churning butter.

"I've been meaning to thank you, Ms. Calleah, for asking your brother to stay away. I've not seen hide nor hair of him in a good week or two." Wendy continued snapping beans.

"I've not seen him either, Miss Wendy. I suspect he's done fallen to his own mischief." She churned the clothes with extra vigor.

Maizie cleared her throat. "Pardon my saying, but Jeremiah said rumors goin' round he done jumped off Devil's Bridge."

Maizie's hands stilled, but Wendy kept working. She didn't want to offend with the comment she could have made.

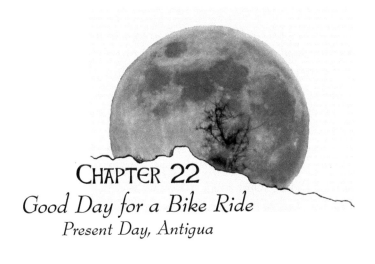

CHAPTER 22
Good Day for a Bike Ride
Present Day, Antigua

"**I** have a surprise for you," I announced, joining Cian on our balcony. The morning sun had yet to reach its heat for the day, so coffee on the balcony while watching Erin ride Iris around the barnyard felt comfortable, if not a mite chilly.

"Oh, aye? Not sure I'm up for any surprises." He took the latte sprinkled with cinnamon from me. I sat in the chair next to his.

"I think you'll like this one. Something we should've done a long time ago. It requires a short bike ride to the other side of town. Are you with me?" I raised my eyebrows at him over my coffee cup.

"Ye don't have a sterling history with bikes, now do ye. You near ran me off a cliff riding to Glass Water Cave. Before that, ye got knocked in a ditch by a truck. Are ye sure you're up to a bike ride? Can ye promise me I'll be safe?" He smirked.

His smirk didn't bother me. I looked out over the sea, hiding my smile in my coffee cup. "Whatever, we will face it together."

A little while later I enjoyed the crunching sound of broken shells under our bike tires, riding down the bungalow drive. Erin sat on Cian's handlebars from our house to the bungalow where Rosa and Emilio lived.

Once upon a time, the bungalow had belonged to me—one of the surprises grand-dad Irish left me when he died. Rosa and Emilio lived with Cian until we married, then they moved into the bungalow to give Cian and I privacy. A perfect choice that kept the bungalow and Shell Cove in the family, and Emilio and Rosa close.

Erin stood on the screened in porch of the bungalow waving to us, getting ready to go swimming at Shell Cove with her grandparents. Her favorite thing to do, other than riding her pony, Iris, that is.

I turned on to the smooth road and kicked into high gear.

"Hey! Wait up! I don't even know where we're going," Cian called after me.

Laughing, I yelled over my shoulder, "Keep up, slow poke!"

The sunshine, island air, the exhilarating wind in my face and hair—I didn't want to slow down. My life had been so dark during the time we searched for Erin. Now we were home, with our precious Erin, safe and sound. All was right with my world. Infused by this energy, I would not slow down. Not today, anyway.

Riding through the town center, I pulled over to a cement picnic table and waited for Cian. "About time you caught up," I said waving him over. "I'm thirsty." I gave him a smile and helped him off with his backpack that held water bottles and grapes.

"Good thing ye got thirsty, else I might never have caught up." He took a long swig of water and popped a couple of grapes in his mouth.

Sweat, or maybe water trickled down his neck. I never tired of looking at my tan, fit husband.

"Irelyn, you're staring at me as if ye could drink me in. Keep it up and I may take ye behind the bushes."

"Sorry, I just never tire of how handsome you are. Just as good looking as the day we married."

"I sure hope so. It's only been seven years." He pulled me into a damp embrace.

"Ooh, you're wet." I pulled away, wiping his sweat off my cheek and arms.

My reaction only made him laugh and rest the backpack on his shoulders again.

I refused to rise to his teasing. I climbed back on my bicycle and led the way across the center of town, going down a couple of blocks to an old wooden church.

Grey wood peeked through the church's peeling, white paint. Tall grasses threatened to overtake the sagging front steps.

"Irelyn, what are we doing at this old church?" Cian followed me, leaning his bike against the steps by mine.

"Around back is the oldest cemetery on the island. When I told our mailman we went to Ireland for great uncle Kyle's funeral, he said his ancestors were buried on the island at old Kincaid's cemetery. Since Mr. Kincaid is the name of the sugar mill owner that purchased your parents, I thought we should check it out. Maybe Wendy is buried here."

A myriad of emotions washed across his face and flickered through his eyes. I took his hand and we walked in silence through the native grasses.

The old building with its peeling paint and sagging foundation appeared weary, as if it had carried the weight of so many sinners for too long. The windows, covered in a dusty film, obscured the view. No longer able to see clearly, the tired church looked like it lost hope and gave itself over to ruin.

A rusty iron fence surrounded the worn tombstones. As unkempt as the building and surrounding yard looked, the graveyard appeared well cared for.

Cian unclasped the gate. "After you, love."

Passing through the gate he held open, I gave him a tentative smile meant to be reassuring. He winked at me without smiling. I guess I wasn't the only one fighting the nerves.

There looked to be about thirty or so tombstones—some crumbling, but a few still stood. Others laid on the ground in pieces covered in moss, making them impossible to read.

"Over here, Irelyn!" Cian knelt next to a stone at the far corner of the yard. "This side over here are the oldest graves. Take a look at this one." He brushed his hand over the crude lettering.

Alexander Kincaid
Beloved Father
Owner of Windy Palms
1618 – 1668

"This must be Wendy's mother next to him." Cian sat back on his heels.

Winerva Kincaid
Wife and Mother
1620 - 1642

"These being the oldest tombstones must be why the church or town named it Kincaid. Mr. Kincaid buried his wife here, then Wendy buried him."

"Wendy must be here too, close by." I stepped over to the next tombstone and dropped to my knees on the cool earth. "Cian, give me your shirt." I held out my hand behind me but did not receive anything. How long did it take to remove a shirt? I peeled my eyes away from the obscured letters to glance up at him.

He stood with his fists on hips, looking at me with one eyebrow raised.

"Please?" I batted my eyelashes at him.

"Oh, all right. I never can resist ye, especially when ye beg." Winking, he took off his shirt and handed it to me.

Rather than comment on his tease, I let it slide and rubbed at the tombstone.

The shirt proved to be pretty ineffectual till Cian took it from me. He wadded the shirt up, spit on it, then gave the lettering a brisk scrub.

"Just needed a little elbow grease…and me shirt." He sat back on his haunches revealing the ancient lettering.

Wendy Kincaid Whitaker
Beloved Wife and Mother
1642 – 1670

"And childhood friend," I said placing my hand on her name.

"And benefactor," Cian siad, adding his thoughts to my own. "She's the reason we have the land we live on." He shook his head. "Seems like just last week she and I sat on a quilt drinking lemonade while I told her of my plan to join you in the future. She didn't even bat an eye."

"She was a good friend. Makes me laugh to remember all the skits we did to entertain her, and the mischief the three of us got into."

"Aye, how about the stories she told? To this day my hairs stand on end remembering the ghost stories she'd tell." He rubbed both his arms like he shivered.

Laughing, I held onto his arm. "Remember when Ms. Calleah asked you to wring a chicken's neck and you couldn't bring yourself to do it?"

"I could too, it's only I couldn't catch the scruffy thing." His face turned a slight shade of red.

His reaction only made me laugh harder. "Then Wendy suggested you try scaring it to death."

"Oh, aye. The two of ye dumped a full bag of confectioners sugar on me head so I'd look like a ghost. The chicken did not drop dead when she saw me, but me mother nearly did!" His own bout of laughter bubbled to the surface. "The horse followed me around, licking me."

I fell back with Cian into the grass, laughing so hard with him I shed tears.

"Oh, Cian, I can still hear your mother fussing. 'Do ye know how long it took me to grind that much sugar in the mortar?'"

"Then up walked Ms. Calleah, scowling with a dead chicken in her hand." His laughter dwindled down to a chuckle. He reached for my hand.

I had no desire but to lie here catching my breath until a shadow crossed over me. Sitting up, I caught a glimpse of a large man walking around the corner of the church building. I only saw the back of him, but the familiarity gave me chills.

"Irelyn? Baby, what's wrong with ye? Me fingers are turning blue, you're gripping me hand so tight."

"Sorry." I released his hand. "I'm sorry, it's nothing. That man looked like...like Cal." I hesitated to say his name. Cal had followed Cian to the present. During our wedding reception he knocked Cian unconscious and took me to Shell Cove at knife point.

His initial desire for the silver coins Cian brought to the present with him changed when he couldn't get them. Instead, he asked for grand-dad Irish's stone from Blarney, thinking he needed it to return to his own time. But I had already returned it to Blarney as Ms. Calleah directed.

105

That night in Shell Cove, under a Blue Moon, the spirit or ghost of my grandmother, as Mira, appeared. Cal, upon seeing her, turned to flee. Falling on his own knife, he shimmered and disappeared. I had always thought he went back to his own time, and most probably died from the knife wound.

Cian scrambled up, jumped over the low fence, and ran to the corner of the building. "There's no one here. Whoever it was, is gone."

"Probably the gentleman that cares for this cemetery popped by and didn't wish to disturb us. I'm just feeling jumpy." Trying to bolster this belief, I gave him a faint smile. "Cian, come back over here and look at the dates on these stones."

He walked back through the iron gate to join me once again. "She died in 1670. So young. Her children must've been mere babes." He shook his head.

"Look at this stone. It must be her husband. Ethan Whitaker. 1640-1670. Do you think they died together?"

"Aye, looks that way. I'd sure like to know what happened."

"Maybe if we research the island's historical archives we can see what happened the year 1670. It may give us a clue as to what happened to the Whitakers—plague, uprising, invasion, that sort of thing. Any of those things would have been recorded."

"Oh, Irelyn, look at this wee one."

On the back of Wendy's stone, the death of what had to be her youngest child was etched.

Christopher Whitaker
1669-1670

"Let's go to the archives tomorrow, Okay?" In need of his touch, I rubbed his arm. Cian had blessed so many lives thus far, surviving a time when life proved too often fleeting.

"Aye, that we will, darling." A glint replaced the sadness in his eyes. I barely had time to wonder before he sprinted toward the gate, calling over his shoulder, "Race ye home!"

CHAPTER 23
Moonbeams and Lullabies
Present Day, Antiqua

"Please, Mommy? Please, Da, can I? It's just right there. You can see me. I want to pet a stingray. I bet they're squishy, or maybe rubbery like a dolphin. Please?" Erin held both hands like a prayer under her chin imploring us.

How could I refuse her, looking into those bright, beseeching eyes? Since returning from Ireland, I waged an inward battle to not become over protective.

Cian and I stood in line for pineapple coconut drinks served in a coconut, which happened to also be something Erin asked for. Cian needed help to carry the drinks, so I couldn't take her.

"All right, Erin." I relented, my hard fought internal battle already lost. "But wait your turn and do not leave the stingray exhibit. Understand? Da and I will bring your drink over."

"Yippie! Thanks, Mommy." She threw her arms around me.

"Don't I warrant a bit of gratitude?" Cian looked askance with his hands on hips.

Erin giggled. "Yes, Da!" She offered him a quick embrace then scurried toward the stingray exhibit.

The island bustled with the afternoon setup for the Carnival festivities. Festivities I almost forgot about until Cian and I came into town this morning to visit the island's historical archives.

Busy crews rushed to set up tents for exhibits and food, bleachers for crowds to watch the opening parade, and stages for the various bands and musicians to perform.

Intending to take Erin to the opening parade, we rushed home to pick her up. The flurry of doing so and getting to the carnival left no time to dwell on the disturbing information unearthed from the archives.

During a French invasion of the island, Windy Palm suffered fire damage, killing Wendy and her youngest baby. Her husband also died during the invasion, defending the plantation. The carnival provided a much needed distraction, allowing me to process the sad news.

A carnival performer, dressed in a day-glo green outfit, had me clutching the coconut drink Cian handed me. His maneuver around the drink line caused him to trip in the tall stilts he wore.

Some people tried to help the performer regain his balance, others scattered to get out of his way. Moving quickly one direction, then another, trying to stay upright, he covered huge lengths of ground with the long poles.

A memory of playing Mother May I as a child popped in my head. I should teach the game to Erin. "Erin! I can't see her! Cian, do you see her?" Panic snapped in like an old friend to tea. How easily I succumbed to the battle.

Cian jumped to action with a drink in both hands. He dodged through the crowd toward the stingray exhibit with me on his heels. A dark-haired boy stood where our daughter had been a moment earlier.

"Erin!" Cian called out, his loud, deep voice causing people to stop what they were doing and stare.

Clutched by fear, I clung to his arm. My heart pounded like one of the steel drums the islanders played. This couldn't be happening again!

"Da? I'm right here. Come feel the stingray!" Erin poked her precious head around a stand-up banner for the exhibit, where she stood petting the slippery skin of a stingray.

Even then my heart struggled to slow its rhythm. I gave Cian a watery smile. He handed me his drink in order to pet the sleek sea creature with his baby girl.

"I'll protect you. I'll be keeping trouble far from where you're sleeping." I tucked a strand of Erin's hair behind her ear. My light touch moved down her forehead, over her yes to encourage her to fall asleep. She'd always been a fan of the song I sang—Dream On by the

Righteous Brothers—and later by the Oakridge Boys. She liked the part about the princess. "You're a princess, chains around you. I'm the hero who just found you." The song never held more meaning for me.

"Irelyn, come on. She's asleep," Cian whispered from the door.

I couldn't help it, I tucked the blanket in a little tighter, as if it could secure her safety, before following my husband up the stairs to the third level of our home. He already lay in bed when I entered the room, holding the covers back for me to slip inside. A moonbeam falling across the floor in front of me from the terrace door made me pause.

"Cian, let's sit outside for a bit. Shall we?"

"I'll get the wine." Just like that, he sprang up and moved to the door. I loved that man.

Bathed in moonlight with my legs folded under me, I took a wine glass from Cian. He took the chair next to me, propping his bare feet on the railing. The quiet between us remained, content to sip our wine and watch the white ocean caps, lit up by the full moon, move across the sea.

Cian's reach for my hand released a deep sigh within me. "Our lassie is going to be okay. We are going to be okay. Everything is all right." I let him clink his glass together with mine.

I couldn't stop one corner of my mouth turning up in what Cian referred to as my half smile. "Now I understand what my mom went through with me. Sometimes—all right, many times—I wish children came with instructions telling us what to do or say. How can God entrust us with something so precious when we have no clue what we're doing?"

Chuckling, he shook his head. "We love our lassie more than life itself. We do our best. Our best is enough."

"I hope you're right."

"Of course, I'm right, aye?" He stood and held a hand out for me. "Come, let's turn in. It's been a long day."

I swallowed the last bit of wine in my glass and let him pull me up, shivering at the wind raising the hairs on my arms.

"Well, now ain't that sweet? The happy, evil couple having a tete-a-tete by the light of the moon. I wanna see that smug, pale face after I take what she loves. Then, I'll kill her too. She'll probably beg me to end her life. It's the least I can do to repay her." Cal muttered to himself, watching Cian and Irelyn from the shadow of a palm tree. He spat on the ground before turning away from the couple who had caused all his misfortunes.

"Irelyn. Irelyn. Wake," a voice said. Without moving I opened my eyes to look about the dark room. Not seeing anyone, I closed my eyes again. I must have dreamed it. I moved closer to Cian.

"Irelyn," The voice said in a deeper, louder voice. This time, knowing myself to be fully awake, I bolted to an upright position. The sound had come from the terrace French doors. I froze. There stood Mira— or "floated" would be more accurate. A more disturbing sight couldn't be found. Her wet, tangled brown hair hung down her white face. The long, tattered dress she wore dripped on the floor. Scratches and cuts covered her arms. Infinite sadness shone from her eyes.

Even though I'd seen her before, and come to no harm, it was quite shocking to be looking at her again. I figured after she helped me defeat Cal when he snatched me on my wedding night, it would be her last appearance. She only seemed to appear to warn me of danger. Danger? Were we in danger? "What is it?" My voice shook with the question.

The ghostly apparition, or spirit, lifted a hand to point outside. "He has returned. He waits." She vanished before my eyes.

The room swirled and I fell back on the pillow. My last conscious thought being, wake Cian. Then all went dark.

"Darling, wake up sleepy head." Cian sat next to me in bed, holding out a cup of coffee. Sun shone through the French doors. Disoriented, I sat up against the headboard and relieved him of the coffee. Scalding my throat with a gulp of the dark liquid, Cian chided me. "Rough night?"

Memory of the visit from Mira flooded my brain. I clutched his arm. "Mira appeared. It's Cal, the man at the cemetery." I spoke in a low voice, not wanting to believe it myself.

"Love, ye've had a bad dream. Who's to blame ye with what we've been through lately, but it cannot be Cal. He's gone, probably died from the knife wound when he returned to his own time. Whether he died or not, he returned to the past."

"Yeah. Yes, I'm sure you're right. It's probably lingering effects of Erin going missing. Maybe my subconscious needs more time to get over our temporary loss of Erin. I'm just having a hard time shaking the feeling of danger."

"Join the living, ye'll feel back to normal soon. It be your turn to fix breakfast. Aye?" He winked at me.

"Smoothies it is, or maybe a bowl of yogurt?" God bless the man that loves a woman such as me. I took another gulp of coffee, before getting up.

CHAPTER 24
Pirates and Lullabies
Antigua 1669

Water lapped at the sides of the rickety 124' wooden ship, Adventure Galley. The old girl, not built well in the first place, had seen better days. She grew weary, much like her Captain, William Kidd, of fruitless searches of the West Indies for pirate ships that might besiege the fairer English ships conducting trade among the islands. Should he find a pirate ship, the English Navy expected him to disable and confiscate it for his own use. Even the treasure or goods aboard he and his crew could keep. Alas, the crew of the Galley had yet to come across any pirate ships, and they grew restless.

"Hoist the sails and set to the oars! The winds have deserted us." Captain Kidd called out to his First Mate. He muttered under his breath, "as has luck."

"Aye, aye, Capt'n."

The sound of oar men rowing below soon started. Captain Kidd watched the massive square sails hoisted by the crew into their rolled position. Three knots under oars is better than sitting still under sail, he thought returning to his quarters.

"Captain! Capt'n! Can ye hear me? There be a Frenchie ship spotted!"

Incessant knocking finally broke through the Captain's rum induced sleep. Upon hearing the words Frenchie ship, he bolted up, attempting to clear the cobwebs from his mind.

The first mate, Cobbs, handed him the spyglass so he could see the

113

French ship for himself. Indeed, there sat a French ship to their port side. It appeared to be anchored off the coast of Antigua.

"What business does a French ship have in Antigua?" The Captain lowered the spyglass.

"Look there, Cap'n. A skiff launched." Cobbs pointed to a long boat pushing out from the French ship.

Once again, he raised the spyglass. "The boat is full of armed soldiers. Doesn't bid well for Antigua." His mouth set in a grim line.

"Maybe not, Cap'n, but it leaves the ship easy pickins for us with their fighters ashore."

Captain Kidd kept silent, considering the situation before him, but that didn't stop Cobbs from continuing.

"Sir, ye know we're due some spoils. The crew has yet to reap any. They're restless and grow more malcontent each day."

"I know it well, Cobbs, but a French ship is not a pirate ship!" He said, his voice even more raspy between clenched teeth. "Hang back til we see what's going on. We may be able to render aid to our countrymen and take the enemy ship. That's an order!"

"Aye." Cobbs kicked the coiled rope at his feet.

Wendy sipped a cup of tea with honey and held a cinnamon scone in her other hand, brought to her by Maizie. She enjoyed a late morning after missing a good portion of sleep due to a teething baby boy during the night. Mmm, nothing smells better than warm cinnamon. She bit into the scone dripping with butter.

Jeremiah's shout under her open window brought the tranquil morning to a halt.

"What in heavens is wrong with the man?" Scowling, she sat down her tea and popped the last bite of scone into her mouth. She flung back the covers and reached for her walking canes. One cumbersome step at a time she made her way down the wooden stairs.

Jeremiah burst through the front door as she reached the bottom. "Mrs.! Oh, Mrs.! It be true! They've come, sure as I'm standing here!" He reached Wendy's side in two long strides and gave her his arm. They walked out onto the covered porch.

She couldn't imagine what had him in such a state. "Who has come, Jeremiah?"

"The frenchies have a ship outside the harbor. Master Ethan asked me to come warn you to make ready for an attack." He sucked in a loud breath. Wendy had not heard so many words from him in one conversation before. "I gots to get all the men workers to go help protect the warehouse with Master Ethan."

Alarmed at the news he brought, her fear centered on Ethan's safety. "Tell him I'll get the women folk inside. We'll hide in the root cellar if need be." She laid a hand on his arm to bring his attention back to her. "Don't worry about Maizie. She knows how to shoot. She and I will both be armed. Please, now hurry. Do your best to see to my husband's safety, will you?" He gave one solemn nod before bounding off the porch.

Watching him run off, she uttered a quick prayer for the safety of Ethan and his men standing guard over Windy Palm Sugar and Rum down at the warehouse across from the harbor.

She sprang into action doing as Ethan requested. Well, as he ordered. Whatever. Ethan knew his wife well. A small smile flitted across her face with these thoughts. Wendy loved her husband beyond words, but he tended to overreact in his overprotective ways. He almost always came around to her way of thinking, but with the French threatening invasion, she feared this was not the time to test her husband. Honestly, she appreciated and relied on his strength in times like these.

The older children were given strict orders to stay in the house. Maizie and Ms. Calleah helped her drag the trunk holding the guns and knives out of Ethan's study, down the hall, through the kitchen, to the back door leading to the root cellar.

Inside the trunk held two Matchlock pistols and one flintlock musket. Maizie and Wendy primed the guns with black powder and loaded the lead ball wrapped in cloth using the ramrod. Now primed and loaded, the guns were put back in the trunk, away from the children. Wendy then made sure all the windows and doors were shut.

Having done all she could to ready for an attack, she had a late lunch prepared and helped her staff play and tell stories to keep the children occupied.

After a long trying day of being shut up in the hot house, for what seemed like no good reason, Wendy relaxed, letting the others move about the house more freely. Ms. Calleah took the children upstairs to the nursery to play so Wendy could rest on her bed.

Too restless to nap, Wendy opened her bedroom window to see if anything was happening down at the harbor. Her eyes widened at a finger of curling black smoke rising to the sky above the palm trees. Shutting the window, she grabbed her walking canes and went to tell Ms. Calleah to take the children downstairs to the kitchen. In the hall Ms. Calleah came out of the nursery jostling baby Christopher on her hip.

"Evening, Miss Wendy. Christopher here, sure is fidgety."

"I'll take him, Calleah. Maybe he'll calm with a little extra nursing. He and I had a long night—what with his teething and a little fever. Hand him to me once I get seated in the rocking chair, would you, please?"

"Sure thing, Miss Wendy. Sometimes the teat is the only thing can calm an edgy babe."

Wendy went back into her room and settled in the cane rocker by the window. Ms. Calleah handed her the squirming baby boy and turned to leave.

"Calleah, it appears the invasion has begun. Take the children down and do as we planned. I'll be down as soon as I nurse this little one. Please tell Maizie it's time to douse the oil lamps. Leave only the one in the cellar. Calleah."

She turned back with a look at Wendy.

"Thank you. We will be all right." She refused to believe otherwise.

"There be a blue moon, Missy. Anything could happen." With a curt nod, she left Wendy to tend the baby.

Settling her son to her breast, she sang a lullaby.

> "Rest sweet baby, close your eyes.
> All is calm. All is calm.
> The lamb lies down with the ewe.
> All is still. All is still.
> Rest sweet baby, close your eyes.
> All is calm. All is calm.
> The colt snuggles closely with the mare.
> All is quiet. All is quiet.
> Hush now baby, rest your head.

All is calm. All is calm.
The chick sleeps under the wing of the hen.
All is well. All is well.
The stars above twinkle in the sky.
Good night. Good night.
Sleep tight."

Whether credit went to the breast milk, the song, the rocking, all three, or simply being in his mother's arms, it worked. Finally, Christopher slept. Exhausted herself, Wendy leaned her head back and joined him in his slumber.

CHAPTER 25
Threats from the Past
Present Day, Antiqua

Inside the blender I dropped strawberries for our morning smoothie. Its loud whir masked the entrance of Erin into the kitchen. Little arms wrapped around my hips. I looked down into her grinning, upturned face. I'll not let any harm come to this child, I thought to myself.

"What shall we add to our smoothie?" Whenever I took my turn at fixing breakfast, smoothies were my go-to. Erin enjoyed adding her own ingredients—usually peanut-butter and bananas.

"Blueberries!"

"Blueberries it is. Get them out of the freezer, please." I could not be more relieved I wasn't adding peanut-butter. I let her push the button on the blender after dropping in a handful of the super fruit.

Pouring our fruity concoction into three glasses, I noticed a new drawing on the fridge. She must've added it when she came in this morning. The picture depicted two figures petting a stingray.

"Nice drawing, Erin. Is that your da?"

"No, Mommy. It's my new friend, Mr. Cal."

The glass slipped out of my hand and shattered on the tile floor, purple liquid spreading out.

"Nobody move," Cian said walking into the kitchen. "Let me pick up the broken bits and wipe up the smoothie first. Blueberries is it?"

Ice made its way down my spine and I shivered. I sat down next to Erin at the kitchen table, putting a hand over hers. Thoughts raced through my head. She's not safe. My baby girl's not safe. He's here! My

119

breath came fast and shallow.

"Irelyn? Love, it's okay. I can clean up the mess. I'll eat a bowl of cereal."

I shook my head. Words escaped me. I pointed to the picture on the fridge.

"Don't you like my picture, Mommy?"

"Of course Ma likes your picture. A lovely drawing it is!" Cian looked at me with his eyebrows drawn.

All I could do was shake my head harder.

Cian continued to stare at me. "Um, Lassie, why don't ye take me phone to the living-room and call your Nanny and Grampy to tell them about petting stingrays?"

I had to follow her—keep her safe. Cian grabbed my hand and pulled me back to the table. I started to object, but he stopped me with a peck on the lips.

"Now, tell me what has you upset. Take a deep breath and let it out slowly. Good."

I didn't want to frighten Erin, so I whispered, "We have to do something, Cian. Cal is here." The muscles in Cian's arms tensed under my hands.

"What makes ye say that? Ye saw him disappear six years ago, and he had a knife injury."

"I know. I know. He must've found a way to come back." At the flicker of doubt in Cian's eyes, I pointed to the proof I'd just found. "Look at Erin's drawing. I assumed it was you with her petting the stingrays." I placed my hand on his cheek, drawing his eyes back to me. "Erin told me it's her new friend, Cal." My voice rasped with emotion, doing my best to keep a whisper.

A crumpled, folded piece of paper fell from my robe.

"What's this?" Cian said stooping to retrieve it.

"Oh, I picked it up off Erin's floor. It's probably one of her drawings."

The tattered paper Cian unfolded made his face turn pale. I grabbed it from him to see for myself why it affected him so. The scrawled note said…

> Irelyn, I see you be well. Not for long.
>
> Not to worry. I no want anything, but I'll take

everything. Should be careful bout letting the brat wander. Somethins bound to happen to her. None to blame but yourself.

"What? How did this get in Erin's room? Cian!" My voice rose with each word.

"We'll figure it out." He grabbed me by the shoulders. "We won't let anything happen to our wee lassie, nor you, even if I have to get you both off the island. Look at me!" He pulled me closer until we stood nose to nose, but even in his arms I couldn't stop trembling. "No one will harm ye. I won't allow it."

Cian's eyes turned dark blue. His normally smiling face looked as if it were chiseled out of stone. Had I just unleashed a dragon? He stormed out of the kitchen without any clue to where he planned to go.

He returned carrying Erin before I even had time to consider following him. Pulling out a chair, he sat her in it. I scrambled to sit in the chair next to hers. He sat across the table from us both.

"Are we going to play a game?" Erin's innocent gaze looked back and forth from her father to me.

"No, Lassie. Mommy and I want to ask you a few questions about your new friend, Cal. Is that okay?"

I held her hand and mustered up a smile for her to put her at ease.

"I finished my yogurt, Da," she said. "Can I go out to ride Iris now?"

"Wait just a minute, lassie. We have a few questions for ye."

With arms spread out wide, Erin threw herself face down on the table. "What now?" she said without turning her head.

Her Da quirked an eyebrow at me while trying to look disapproving. "Your Ma found this note on your floor. Who gave it to ye?"

At least she made the effort to glance at the note. "Oh, a friend of Mommy's. He petted the stingray with me while the tall man wobbled all around." She giggled.

"What did he say, Sweetheart?" The desperation inside me made it difficult to keep the alarm out of my voice.

"Umm. He said he's a friend of yours and could I give you a note. Then he said he'd see me around." She flipped over to her back.

"Did he tell ye his name, lassie?"

"Yep, Cal. Can I go now?"

121

Biting the inside of my lip, I gave Cian a see-I-told-you-so look.

"Yes, lass. I'll go with ye so ye can show me that new trick uncle Jorge taught ye."

Sonja and Jorge came over at our urging to pick up Erin, giving Cian and I the time and freedom to discuss the Cal situation in private. Thankfully, it didn't require much urging to get them to come. Auntie and Uncle, as Erin called them, loved spending time with their only niece. Although there was no blood relation between us, they were family all the same. They would keep a close eye on her.

Cian and I were alarmed when Erin told us Cal knew her pony, Iris, and that's how she knew he was a friend. He told her he comes by to say hi to Iris every now and then, and someday soon he'd come to see her too. I became so lightheaded at her words, Erin looked at me funny and said, "You look like a ghost."

Sitting at the round kitchen table, I wrung my hands. Cian paced across the kitchen floor. The gentle breeze blowing in the window over the sink a huge contrast to the tense atmosphere in the room.

"What are we going to do? Should we call the police?" I said, watching him go back and forth.

"I considered that, but what would we tell them? We think there's a man from the past stalking our wee daughter?"

"You're right. They wouldn't do anything until she disappeared. It wouldn't hurt to give them a description of Cal so they could keep a lookout, though."

"Right ye are, love. We'll do that, but I think we need to handle this ourselves. We need to get him back to his own time and make sure he stays there!" Cian stopped pacing and pounded a fist into his palm.

I couldn't disagree, but how would we do it? "Any idea on how we accomplish such a feat?"

"Aye, well, our cove appears to be amenable to time travel." Again, he tramped back and forth. "We can lure him there during a blue moon and send him back." My lack of response had him glancing my way on another pass by. "Well, what do ye think?"

"What I think is," I said catching his hand and pulling him toward the table, "you're going to wear a path in my kitchen floor. Besides, I can't concentrate with you going back and forth incessantly."

He pulled out a chair and sat down. Sitting across the table from me, our held hands brought added strength and calmness to me.

"I like your plan. We should consider how far away the next blue moon is. Also, how will we ensure he doesn't return to our time?"

We had much to discuss and plans to work out. The process took us straight through the remainder of the morning and into the afternoon as well.

Erin burst through the door followed by Sonja and Jorge. Our almost always exuberant daughter slowed down only enough to wave at us as she dashed by. Her high spirits fetched a welcome smile.

Still smiling, I welcomed Sonja and Jorge. "Come, let's sit in the living-room. I've spent more than enough time in this kitchen today."

"Gladly! Jorge and I have an idea to put by the two of you."

"Well then, I'd better get us all a glass of tea." I moved to the cabinet for glasses. The others continued to the living-room.

Joining them with a tray of glasses filled with tea, I passed each one out and sat next to Cian on the couch. The love they had for my daughter exuded with every word they used to fill us in on their day with Erin.

"Wait, what did you say?" Sonja's round eyes looked incredulous. "Jorge, did she just say Erin can go to Virginia with us?"

"That's what I heard, Babe." Jorge looked just as shocked.

Their reactions brought laughter to my lips. "Yes, why not? I think it'll be good for her. She's been feeling a bit coddled lately. It's so sweet of you to want her along. She's going to be so happy."

"You know we love our little pony riding princess. I'm so excited! Come on, Jorge, we've got to go home and procure her ticket." She gave Jorge a hand, pulling him to his feet. Not giving either Cian or I time to stand, she leaned over and hugged us both. "Bye! Let's go Jorge."

"Later, guys." Jorge waved and allowed himself to be pulled toward the door, a smile plastered on his face.

Their enthusiastic exit made me chuckle. I smiled at Cian. "That couldn't have worked out better if we'd planned it ourselves."

"As soon as their plane lifts off we can safely get to work on our plan. Come here, ye look mighty kissable." He pulled me against him, putting one hand on the back of my head and the other at the small of my back. I glimpsed the flame of desire in his eyes before his lips lowered to mine. I closed my eyes and opened my lips to his, warming myself in his fire.

Sonja and Jorge's trip to Virginia would take care of some staff issues with the school that she and I opened together after graduating from the university.

They offered to take Erin to Virginia with them, to give Cian and I some time to focus on each other after the ordeal we lived through when our daughter went missing in Ireland. They thought a little time alone together, where Erin wasn't our sole focus, would do us good… little did they know.

A week later, Cian and I said goodbye to Erin, Sonja, and Jorge at the airport. Lucky for us, this year would bring two blue moons in a single year. Something that only happens four or five times in a century! I was counting on the Blue Moon to help us send Cal back to his own time. Our very own cove seemed to have something to do with time travel as well, seeing as how it was the place Cian used to travel here, and also Cal.

Keeping Erin indoors for a week proved to be trying. Cian took her out to care for her pony, Iris, daily. Usually, they'd go for a ride between our property and Emilio and Rosa's, but until we neutralized the threat from Cal, Cian kept her rides in the corral. Our adventurous Erin did not like the limits set on her. It made saying goodbye at the airport a little easier. She would get a good dose of adventure with Uncle Jorge and Aunt Sonja.

"Our wee bird needed to spread her wings a little," Cian said.

Smiling, I waved at her with only a little extra wetness to my eyes. She skipped away, holding Sonja's hand.

At home I threw together some lunch and took it and ice tea to our private third floor balcony. Here I felt safe, with Cian beside me. A place to enjoy the view and the soft island breeze. Later in the day our plan would be in full swing.

Thinking about what lay ahead raised goosebumps on my arms. No amount of island breezes could chase that chill away, especially when I spied a lone figure standing at the back corner of the barn. Unmoving, he stood there watching the yard until finally he crept alongside the barn. At the wide doors he yanked the note off that Cian had tacked to the barn door. Cian figured by placing it there he wouldn't miss it, and he didn't.

It brought mixed emotions for me. Although relieved that he saw the note, it confirmed he indeed watched us. This confirmation left me all the more determined for our plan to succeed. He never once raised his eyes beyond the yard. A smile tugged at the corner of my mouth remembering a saying Grandad Irish used. "A few sheep short of a flock."

In the note he took...

Ye seek revenge for your own misdeeds.
To trouble this will lead.
The past calls ye home.
Come to the cove, ye won't be alone.
Within an hour of the first light of the moon,
We will be there. This will end soon.

Hoped spurred me forward, along with the 9mm Walther I carried back to the kitchen. The gun wasn't loaded. Inherited from my dad, I'd never even bought bullets for it.

Cian leaned against the copper sink holding a small suede drawstring bag containing fifty-two quarters, state quarters, to be exact. We had enjoyed collecting each one with Erin.

The plan involved a bribe for Cal to return to the past with the bag of coins. The trick would be making him think the bag contained the silver coins Cian brought with him from the past. The gun was for extra incentive. Speaking of the gun...

"Did you know a Walther is the gun James Bond carried?"

"Oh, aye? Who be James Bond?"

I opened my mouth to explain, but realized it would take far too long, and even then he might not understand. I shook my head. "Never mind."

"Oh, an old suitor is he?" He quirked an eyebrow at me.

Maybe I could blame it on nervous energy, but his assumption put me in stitches.

My laughter only made him frown. He snatched up the gun and tucked it in his waistband. "I don't see what ye find so funny, Irelyn. I expect ye had more than one suitor while ye resided in Virginia."

A deep breath quieted the laughter bubbling inside me. I sidled up next to him and laid my head on his broad shoulder. "I'm not laughing at you. Sorry, your comment had me envisioning myself as a Bond Girl."

"A what girl? Never mind, let's get to the cove." He kissed me on the head before moving away to slide the door open.

With our beach quilt in hand, I preceded him out the door to what we called our verandah.

CHAPTER 26
Soldiers and Pirates
Antigua 1669

Ethan watched French soldiers pull their small wooden boats ashore from the safety of the warehouse. He and his men had the warehouse locked up tight, and stood guard with guns and knives ready. He pushed thoughts of Wendy and their young'uns aside to focus on the danger at hand.

When the cutter flying the French flag sailed into the harbor, he sent Jeremiah to warn Wendy to take precautions. He trusted she had the good sense the Lord gave her to heed his warning when it mattered.

Flames shot up, lighting up the dusk sky. The French were torching the other boats and ships docked in the harbor. Their motive to probably draw the men of the island to the docks, leaving the warehouses and plantations easy prey.

Ethan shouted to his men to remain posted and stay watchful. A few of them nodded with their eyes wide. Most had never faced such a situation. They gripped their weapons with white knuckles. He uttered a quick prayer for their safety.

A feral yell jolted him to attention. A group ran toward the warehouse.

"Fire!" Ethan commanded his men to shoot the French soldiers rushing to them.

Shots rang out, deafening his hearing. The two opposing forces clashed together with flashing blades.

The oil lamp cast peculiar shadows on the walls. Maisie sat huddled on the dirty floor of the cellar patting Benjamin's back so the fretful child would fall asleep on his pallet.

Ms. Calleah sat on a wooden stool rocking little Aisley. She hummed a lilting tune to calm the girl.

"Don't you reckon I should check on Mrs. Whitaker?" Maisie whispered to Ms. Calleah.

"No," Ms. Calleah said. "She'll be down soon enough. She be nursing the baby."

Hearing the kitchen door slam, followed by thudding footsteps, the two women stared at each other, wide eyed. Neither dared to breathe lest they be heard.

They gasped in unison when the door flung open, and a large, dark figure barreled down the steps. He stepped into the dim light, revealing his rugged face. The women let out a collective breath.

"Jeremiah! What do you mean scaring us like that? You're disturbing the little ones!" Maisie scowled at him. Ms. Calleah looked at him expectantly.

"Don't you smell smoke, woman? This here plantation is burning down around you while you're going on about me being a disturbance. I'm trying to save your ungrateful self!"

"Jeremiah!" Ms. Calleah bellowed. "Stop your fussing and kindly tell us what's happening so we know what to do."

"Right. Sorry about that. Me and Mister Ethan, and the warehouse workers stood guard outside the warehouse. The Frenchies came ashore and went right to setting the docked boats to flame. Mister Ethan, he yelled for us to stay put. Next thing you know we was set upon by a bunch of 'em, hollering like banshees. We felled several of 'em. Then, I seen Mister Ethan chase after some of 'em that looked to be headed in the direction of the plantation. So, I chased after Mister Ethan. I never did catch up to him, and the sugar cane fields are torched. I fear what's befell him."

"They'll more'n likely loot and burn this fine house next. We best get the children somewhere safe. Quickly!" Ms. Calleah scooped up little Aisley like she weighed no more than a bushel of apples. Jeremiah picked up Benjamin and set him on his feet.

The little group of five climbed the stairs and opened the kitchen door to be engulfed in billowing smoke and embers raining down from the ceiling. Screaming, Aisley hid her face in Ms. Calleah's skirt. She ushered her outside, clutching tight to Benjamin's hand.

Huddled together on the front lawn, Ms. Calleah scanned the yard for Wendy. "Mistress Wendy. Wendy! Sweet Jesus, where's my Wendy?" She turned in circles seeking a glimpse of Wendy's slight frame through the haze.

"You don't think she still be upstairs?" Maisie wrung her hands.

"No. Nooo!" Ms. Calleah cried over and over.

Two more of Ethan's men fell, their cause to save the warehouse from the French becoming a lost one. A band of soldiers sprinted past on the inland road, heading toward the plantation.

He head-butted his adversary. The dazed man fell backward. Ethan used the opportunity to follow the soldiers inland. Fear for the warehouse replaced by fear for Wendy and their three children.

Cursing the light of the full moon, he ran the well-trod path. A path he could run from warehouse to plantation blindfolded, having walked or rode it daily. Now the traitorous moon lit the way for the soldiers, easing their way.

Ethan slowed almost to a stop. The men no longer seemed to be ahead of him. In fact, they were nowhere to be seen nor heard.

A burst of light blinded him. He raised his hands up to his forehead to shield his eyes from the light, feeling a slick wetness there. Before he could make sense of what happened, he tumbled to the ground. His head barely missed a rock that showed a telltale spot of blood. The full moon slipped behind the clouds, Ethan's world going dark.

"Wendy," escaped his lips on a breath before he lost all consciousness.

In the deep waters outlying the harbor the crew of the Adventure Galley grew restless, the deckhands pacing. The Quartermaster kept watch through the only spyglass.

"What be happening, Mate? I'm telling you, those French curs be up to no good!" Robby growled.

"Look! There's smoke!" Hanging over the side, Paly pointed toward the island.

Lowering the spyglass, Quartermaster Cobbs said, "Yep. Looks to me they're burning the sugarcane while looting the warehouses. Aw, such a waste of fine timber."

"What? What else?" Yelled the sailmaster, Robby.

"They set fire to the other boats and ships. A strategic move, to be sure." He shook his head.

"Robby, go fetch the Captain. He'll want us to render aide, I'm thinking."

"The Captain's right here!" Captain Kidd hopped down the last couple of steps to join his agitated crew on deck. "The Quartermaster's right. Weapon up, men, and lower the boats. We're joining the fight!"

A cheer rippled through the ship. The men hurried off to ready themselves for much awaited conflict.

Chuckling to himself, Captain Kidd thought, bet the French soldiers aren't expecting to be set upon by pirates to aide the island and foil their raid, but that's what's going to happen.

The crew rowed to the shallows and waded to shore in no time at all. One party set off to the cane fields to stop further destruction. Another lot stayed at port, engaging soldiers who attempted to load captured slaves, rum, and sacks of sugar into boats. Of course, as reimbursement for their "good deed," they kept a fare amount of rum and sugar for their own use.

Following the acrid smell and glowing orange sky, the band of twelve pirates came upon French soldiers. Robby thought the soldiers must be feeling secure in the fact that the slaves had been rounded up and the plantation owners subdued. They stood watching fire make waste of the cane fields. Laughing and talking among themselves, they showed no awareness of the company of pirates now flanking them on both sides and to their rear.

Robby shot the soldier still holding a torch to get their attention. There were other ways of gaining attention, but this one sent a clear message they weren't playing around. He reasoned it saved lives overall. The other men dropped their weapons and put their hands on top of their heads, following Robby's instructions.

Grinning, the cocky pirate led the captives back to the coast with smoke and flames continuing to rise at their backs. Little could be done about the fires anyway.

CHAPTER 27
Dangerous Liasons
Present Day, Antigua

O n top of the rock Cian once buried his silver coins under, I considered how so much of our history involved this large mainstay. The place where we even reunited as adults after not seeing one another since childhood. A smile broke out on my face remembering Cian stepping out from behind the rock wearing nothing but a towel.

"What do ye find so amusing?"

"Just remembering how fine you look in a towel."

"Aye? Well, now as soon as we return to the house, I'll model one for ye." He sat cross legged beside me, hitting a coconut against the rock.

"Shouldn't you be saving your energy to deal with Cal?"

"I'll have this cracked open in no time. I'll still have plenty of energy to handle that snake, and some to spare for ye, love."

One more slam against the rock and the coconut cracked open. He winked at me and lifted it to his mouth for a drink of the watery milk.

Turning my back to him, I eased down, laying my head in his lap to watch the first stars of the evening appear in the dusk sky. The soft, steady sound of the tide edging ever closer helped calm my jangled nerves. Our plan had too many holes, making me apprehensive over Cian's safety. Cal had knocked him unconscious once before on our wedding night. I sure didn't wish a repeat of those harrowing events. Thankfully, Cian interrupted my disturbing thoughts trying to act against the lulling of the sea.

"Irelyn, don't ye think it strange mosquitos don't seem to like our cove? Everywhere else I've been on the island, the wee buggers abound—but not here. Why do ye think that is?"

"Honestly, I've never noticed, but they're always attracted to you more so than me. I guess I'm not as likely to notice their absence as—"

Cian's muscles tensed underneath me. Without saying a word, he helped me sit up. He uncrossed his legs and pushed himself off the rock to stand in front of it, and me.

Searching the spot where the path opened into the cove, I looked for Cal. Not seeing anyone, or anything out of the ordinary, I started to breathe again. Then, out of the shadows stepped Cal.

With his ever present sneer in place, he opened his mouth to speak. But Cian beat him to it.

"Ye don't belong in this time." Cian and I had agreed during planning that Cian should be the one to direct the conversation, rather than allow Cal to push our buttons. "Go back to yer sister, and stay there, or things will go poorly for ye." He put his hand on the gun at his hip.

Cal snickered. "Things were going poorly for me back then. I got no one there. Cali's too busy being a nurse wipe for Miss Wendy's brats to be concerned with me. The way I sees it, here I got endless enjoyment making the two of you suffer. Besides, I'd miss my pretty little friend. Someone's gotta teach her the ways of the world. Lately she's not been riding her pony. You lock her up or something?"

The way Cian's hand tightened around the gun, I figured I'd better speak up. "We have silver coins! We'll give you our bag of silver if you go back to stay."

He grew quiet. I could almost see the conniving thoughts running through his thick skull. Coming here had been a mistake. Nothing would stop him from taking our money and returning to our time the next Blue Moon. What would we do then?

Cian must have read Cal's expression the same as I. He shifted from being a shield in front of me to standing toe to toe with Cal. He moved so fast, I couldn't have stopped him.

He shoved the bag of coins into Cal's gut. Moonlight gleamed upon the barrel of the gun Cian held to Cal's Chest. Cal grunted but grabbed the bag. He slipped it into his pocket with one hand while the other arm executed a block, knocking the gun out of Cian's hand. Cian responded by throwing an elbow to Cal's jaw.

Frozen in place, I couldn't tear my eyes away from them until they fell to the sand, fists flying. I scrambled down off the rock but had to stop to rub sand from my eyes. The wind had whipped up something fierce. Holding one arm across my eyes, I stumbled over to where the men wrestled on the ground.

The air crackled as if charged with electricity. I dropped to my knees to pull them apart only to have a wet palm frond slap me in the face. Only then did I notice the rain.

I grabbed hold of Cian's arm but the cove began spinning. It spun so fast, I keeled over next to the men who had grown still. No matter how much I struggled, I couldn't raise my head. The moonlight around us brightened. Helpless, I shut my eyes against the spinning.

"Irelyn. Irelyn, wake up! Please, love."

I woke to Cian shaking me. "Did you burn the bacon again? Let me sleep a little longer. Then I'll help you."

"What? No, I didn't burn the bacon. That's only ever happened one time. Irelyn, the sugar cane fields are burning! Come, now. We must help Wendy!"

"But we don't have a sugar cane field. Wendy? Wendy!" My eyes popped open wide. I sat up. We were outdoors, then I remembered why. "Cal! Where's Cal? Are you all right?" Grabbing Cian by his shirt front, I scanned his face and head for bumps, bruises, or blood.

"I'm fine. Really, I am. Cal wasn't here when I woke up. Can't be sure he travelled back, but we'll find out." He took my hand and looked me in the eye. "Irelyn, remember how Wendy and her babe died? I fear it's tonight. We may be too late, but we must hurry to check on her. Do ye reckon yer ready to get moving now?"

"Yes, yes, of course!"

Pulled to my feet a smoky haze attacked my lungs. I crouched right back down and Cian joined me. I pulled my shirt up over my nose. Cian did the same with his shirt and grabbed my hand with his only free one.

"The house is this way." He kept my hand clasped in his. His breathing sounded as labored as mine through the material but neither of us pulled our shirts away from our noses.

Large banana leaves brushed against me in our run down the dirt path toward the house, following the sound of wailing. Breaking out into the open, I caught sight of the main house set ablaze. Ms. Calleah and two children, as well as a couple of people who I assumed were servants stood on the front lawn.

Ms. Calleah wailed along with the children, crying out for their momma. The large, African man held an empty bucket. We sprinted the distance to inquire of Wendy's whereabouts.

"Oh, heavens! The Lords done sent me an angel!" Ms. Calleah grabbed Cian by the arm.

"Where's Wendy? Tell me where she is!"

Wailing again, Calleah pointed to an upstairs room. Cian started for the front steps, but the man stopped him.

"Sir, she can't be reached. The stairwell is in flames. I tried dousing it with water from the well, but the stairs are still burning."

"Is there a ladder?"

"Yes, Sir. In the barn around back." Looking downcast, he said, "I shoulda thought of it, myself."

Cian tore out around the corner of the house. I got as close to the house as I dared and yelled for Wendy. It looked like we were too late, for surely she would be at the window trying to get out or get fresh air.

My determined husband returned with a wooden ladder. The man held it steady against the house for Cian to scale it. I tried to reassure the young girls, watching him climb.

At the top of the ladder, he bent over and took off a shoe to break the window. Smoke billowed out like storm clouds moving across the water. Cian reached in to lift the latch and raise the window. Even in fear for his safety, my heart swelled with pride and awe watching him climb into a burning house with the slim hope of rescuing a friend.

Time seemed to stretch for eternity waiting for him to reappear. Had part of the ceiling fallen on him? Had the smoke overcome him? Did his body lay on the other side of the window while I did nothing but watch for his return?

Unshed tears gathered in my eyes when a bundle of white sheets appeared on the window sill in the arms of Cian. My heart leapt, my whole being loving that man.

"Irelyn, come quickly! I'm going to lower the babe down to ye in the sheet."

Standing below the window, I held my arms up for the baby, who should've been crying. As soon as I had a hold of him, Cian dropped the sheet and disappeared again. Immediately, I lay the child on the ground to administer CPR—all the while trying to recall the infant CPR Training I received while expecting Erin. Good thing all that training took over. I pushed using two fingers on his chest then breathed, covering his nose and mouth. The beautiful baby boy gasped for air, coughed, wheezed, and let out a hoarse cry. So pleased with myself, I laughed.

Ms. Calleah swooped in like a mama bird and scooped him up. Walking around the yard, she cradled him murmuring unintelligible words.

So intent on reviving the baby boy I missed my dashing, daring husband climb out of the two story window. He worked his way down the ladder with a seemingly lifeless Wendy thrown over his shoulder.

At the bottom rung, Jeremiah relieved him of Wendy's body. He gently laid her in the grass, smoothed the hair from her brow and bowed his head.

Laying a hand on the large man's shoulder, Cian said, "Jeremiah, Wendy lives. Look, she's breathing. Slow, shallow breaths, but breathing all the same."

Maizie dropped to her knees next to Wendy with Aisley at her head. Benjamin held his mother's hand while Maizie rubbed Wendy's arm.

Aisley placed her tiny hands on either side of her mama's face and leaned over her. "Breathe, Mommy."

The clouds covering the full moon burst open, releasing a deluge of rain, exactly what the burning house and fields needed. Wendy must have needed it too, for she sucked in air, rolled over and began coughing. Maizie pounded on her back while Benjamin and Aisley covered her in kisses. Sitting up, with help from Cian, Wendy took notice of his presence.

"Cian?" she whispered. "Am I dreaming? Are you really here? What about Irelyn? Did you find her?"

Laughing, Cian answered all her questions. "Aye, I'm really here. Irelyn and I are married. We even have a wee lassie. Irelyn's here as well. Rest and we'll talk more tomorrow. I have some business to tend to."

"Thank you for saving my life." Wendy pulled him down to kiss him on the cheek. "I've missed you." Holding a hand out to Irelyn, she called for her. "Get over here right this minute! Oh, my, you've grown into a beautiful woman. You were such a cheeky little girl. I missed you so after you left. Cian did his best to keep me entertained, but it just wasn't the same without his sidekick. Not to be stingy, but I do hope you and Cian are staying. Where's your daughter? Did she travel with you?" Wendy scanned the yard.

"No, she's not here. We'll tell you all about it tomorrow. I fear it's a long story in the telling, especially in the rain. I'm so glad to see you too."

Wendy's children demanded her attention, so I stood and backed away to accommodate them.

I'm sure I looked like a wet dishrag, but I didn't care. We had saved Wendy and her precious baby boy, and the rain kept the house from being a total loss. Flinging my arms out, palms up to the rain, I recognized the blessing of the rain. Cian grabbed me around the waist and swung me around.

Aisley chased Benjamin around Wendy, who now held tightly to baby Christopher. Other than a hoarse voice and a lingering cough, the two of them appeared to be fine.

The large man, and Maizie stood arm in arm, with big grins on their faces, watching the children chase each other around. Calleah sat in the grass next to Wendy, patting her back.

"Jeremiah, is the barn burnt to the ground, or can we take shelter there for the night?" Wendy said to the large man, loud enough to be heard above the children's squeals and the rain.

"No, Ma'am. The barn be fine. The fire didn't make it that far. Let me help you to it. We can make do with the horse blankets and hay for the time being." Jeremiah squatted down and lifted Wendy with her baby into his strong muscled arms like she weighed no more than a two stringed bale of hay. He carried her off to the barn with the girls, Maizie and Ms. Calleah in tow.

I started to follow but Cian raised his arm to block my way. "We must try to locate Cal so we can determine if he travelled back when we did."

"You're right. With all the excitement I forgot all about Cal. Where should we look?" I wiped the moisture off my face, though a futile action with the amount of rain falling, trying to stifle a yawn.

"Ye know, I think maybe ye should stay with Wendy and her wee laddie to ensure they suffer no ill effects from the smoke inhalation. I'll ask Jeremiah to go with me. We can look for Wendy's Ethan too." At my frown he pulled me to him, locking his arms around my middle with his forehead to mine. "I know ye would rather go with me, but I'd rather ye didn't encounter Cal. Sorry, but I may need Jeremiah's brute strength." He kissed the tip of my nose. I didn't argue, for in truth, I didn't feel up to an encounter with Cal.

Inside the barn Jeremiah gladly agreed to go with him. He had probably had enough of female company.

Cian took the knife Jeremiah handed him, tucking it into his waistband at his back. He hoped they didn't encounter any French troops. Getting captured and carted off to France certainly wouldn't make Irelyn happy, nor did it fit into his plan of returning to the life he had with Irelyn and Erin.

Moving with stealth, he and Jeremiah followed the path toward the harbor. The rain stopped, making it easier for the men to see, and leaving a fresh botanical scent to the air.

The sight of the scorched sugar cane fields his father, Brian, had devoted much of his life to made him frown. His father had served the Windy Palm Plantation owner, Mr. Kincaid as his manager. He had taken pride in his work. Cian loved following him around as a child, learning how to work the sugar mill.

Lost in his memories, he almost walked right past a man lying deathly still on the side of the dirt path. Jeremiah gasped and knelt close to the man, lifting his head onto his legs. Judging Jeremiah's reaction, this man must be Wendy's Ethan.

Working together, Cian felt for a pulse while Jeremiah tore off a strip from his coarse cotton shirt and tied it as a bandage around Ethan's head. He looked deathly pale and a bloody puddle of water sat where his head had laid.

Using hand signals, they agreed to carry him back to the barn. His wound needed to be cared for, the French situation in the harbor and Cal would just have to wait.

One would never guess Wendy herself had almost died too. The moment they entered the barn she went to work making a comfortable spot for her husband. She sent Caleah to her hut for supplies to cleanse and close the wound.

"We're going to the harbor to see if the French have left, and look for Cal."

"Please be careful, love." I wrapped my arms around his neck and kissed him soundly on the mouth.

"So far, we haven't come across any troops, or anyone at all except for Ethan. It's as if everyone is gone. It's a little eerie."

His words made me shiver. I watched them hurry down the path until the night swallowed them both.

Cian's knees grew stiff crouching behind an upturned rowboat. He and Jeremiah watched the soldiers march slaves to the French boats. I grow too old for these adventures, he thought to himself.

He sensed Jeremiah's tension beside him. The large man seemed about to spring to his fellow slaves aide. Cian laid a hand on his arm to stay him. He pointed to a crew of what appeared to be pirates. The motley band of men engage the soldiers and free the slaves. All but one of the slaves wasted no time in making off in various directions.

The one remaining slave, drew a knife from his boot and stabbed a French soldier. The soldier crumpled to the ground, triggering several pirates to run forward. But when they tried to apprehend the attacker, he turned on them too. He raised the knife like he intended to throw it at one of the pirates. A fired shot dropped the slave, cold. Nonplussed, the pirates continued about their tasks.

Something about the man captured Cian's attention. Crouching as he went, he moved from the rowboat to a cluster of palmettos, about a hundred feet closer to the man on the ground.

The man wore blue jeans. He saw people in jeans all the time, so it didn't immediately register as abnormal, but in the 1600s jeans had yet to be invented. Cian wondered if it could be Cal. They'd have to wait for the pirates to leave before taking a closer look. He scurried back to Jeremiah and the two of them went to inspect the Windy Palm warehouse.

A couple of Ethan's men died defending the warehouse against the French. However, it remained standing, untouched by fire. The place looked like the pirates had helped themselves to barrels of sugar— refined and powdered—crates of bottled rum, and molasses. It looked like there remained enough stores for Ethan and Wendy to get by on profitably. The pirates had saved the day, after all.

Outside the warehouse no pirate or French ship remained anchored in or near the bay. Cian jogged across to where the man had been shot down.

"Bless me, it be Cal!" Cian said.

Chapter 28
Ethan and Wendy
Antigua 1669

"Watch, Mommy! I can walk up the wishing steps backward all by myself. The Druid King has to grant my wish. Right, Mommy? Right?" Erin climbed one step at a time with her nose scrunched up and her eyes closed tight. My mouth moved, but no sound came out. I had to stop her! Taking a deep cleansing breath to calm myself, I opened my mouth to try again.

"Stop!" I said, my voice barely above a whisper. I held my hand up, begging her to stop, but her eyes were closed.

"Irelyn! Wake up, love, ye be dreaming again."

I awoke disoriented from Cian's gentle shake on my shoulder. The barn loft surroundings, unfamiliar at first, snapped me into a sitting position. I found bits of straw caught in my hair, but also remembered Wendy and her children, along with Maizie, Jeremiah, and Caleah who spent the night below the loft.

Other than the children, I doubt any of them got much sleep, for they had planned to take turns caring for Ethan and his severe concussion. Wendy deemed Cian and I unfit to take a turn. Of course we did struggle to not sway on our feet last night. Time travel tended to be a good sleep aid.

The extra swipe it took to remove the sleep from my eyes only revealed my handsome husband staring at me. "Tell me, why do I keep dreaming about Erin and The Wishing Steps?"

Chuckling, Cian shook his head. "Beats me, but your dreams usually mean something. Remember how your grandmother kept telling you

141

not to forget about the irises in your dreams, and a box with her diary turned up buried beneath the irises?"

"Yes, well, I'm not so sure that was a dream. Has Erin ever told you what she wished for?"

"No, but I think it's time we found out." He stood and pulled me to my feet. "Let's join the others and see what we can do to help out."

"Okay, but then let's talk to Calleah about when we can hope to get home. I know Erin is safe with Sonja and Jorge, especially now that we know Cal is no longer a threat. Still, I'll feel better once I know we are able to return home."

"Aye, me too."

"Join us, you sleepy heads!" Wendy said stirring a tall pot of oatmeal in the yard. Grab a cup and help yourself." She pointed beyond where she sat. "There's fresh butter over there, and the tastiest molasses in the West Indies."

"Wendy, who are all these people?" I said.

Tin cup in hand, Cian ladled himself an ample portion of the hot oats. I looked around at men and women sitting on the lawn eating. My stomach grumbled.

"The land and shop owners of the island gathered this morning to discuss the damage. We all agreed the best and quickest way to recover is to all work together on each other's property. We cast lots to determine whose would be first and we won! I figured the least I could do was feed them breakfast." She winked at me, continuing to stir. "Folks work better on a full stomach."

Filling a cup for myself, I added butter and molasses before joining Cian. "Cian, I'd like to visit your ma and da's graves while we're here." I looked at him under the cover of my lashes, hoping my words didn't upset him. Their deaths were far more recent for him.

"Sure thing, love. Glad I am ye wish to see them, for I do, too. Maybe we can get away for a bit today." He smiled at me before putting another bite of oatmeal in his mouth.

Repairs for the burned portion of the roof and burned stairs took much of the day. Once the plantation house stood firm and livable again, the men moved on to the next building in need of repair.

The women stayed behind to see to the cleanup. All the curtains were taken down for washing, and the walls and floors needed scrubbing. Eventually, even the walls would be repainted.

By the time the moon rose in the sky, Ethan, Wendy, Cian, and I sat around the outdoor firepit sipping cups of rum made at Windy Palm.

Wendy filled Cian in on the changes at the sugar mill since he'd left. Ethan regaled us with tales of courting Wendy, and dealing with her father, Mr. Kincaid, who considered no one worthy of his only daughter.

Ethan held up his right hand. "I testify, if I were the crown prince of England, Mr. Kincaid, God rest his soul, would not have found me worthy of his little princess."

"Princess?" Wendy's eyebrows raised, but her lopsided smile kept her far from looking upset. "Then, they were my court jesters!" She pointed to Cian and me.

Once Cian stopped laughing enough to speak, he said, "Aye, to be sure we were. There be none sillier than we two were, trying to keep ye entertained." He reached out and put an arm around me, the laughter dying around us.

"What happened to your father, Wendy?" The island's historical archives had offered no insights to answer this question.

"He didn't come to breakfast one morning." She shrugged her slight shoulders. "You know father, he never missed breakfast. We found him still in bed. The doctor said it looked like he suffered apoplexy."

"I'm so sorry. There's no other as generous as he lived."

"Aye, he was a good man," Cian added.

"Maizie and Jeremiah came to be at Windy Palm because of Father's goodness. I'll tell you the story I've heard him tell many times. I won't be able to tell it as well, mind you.

One moon-beaming bright night, the sleepless malaise struck him hard. Knowing it to be relentlessness, he determined to get some fresh air with the hope he'd be able to sleep upon returning. The moon lit the island as if it were only dusk instead of the dead of night. So, he rode Sable to the shore to see the sea spray and spume fly up, glowing white in the moonlight out of Devil's Bridge. He said he imagined, rightly so, it'd be a sight to behold—stunning. Father would stop in his telling here to point a finger at the listener. 'Now, I don't recommend you ever

143

try such foolishness. People don't call it the Gates of Hell for nothing. The devil himself resides there, spitting at folks that dare walk close, but I've never been one to let my good sense get in my way.' My mind's eye can still see him wink."

Wendy mimicked her father's voice perfectly. "'Sable is the best horse I've ever owned. You could say she has better sense than I do, because when the spray fell back to the ground, there stood two dark skinned people huddled together. For a second all that showed were their round white eyeballs staring up at me. Sable reared up, knocked me to the ground, and off she tore back to the barn. I knew there could only be one reason for the two of them standing at Hell's Gate. Truly, it's a wretched circumstance that causes any of God's creations to aspire to end their own life. Many slaves have been driven to do the deed at Devil's Bridge.' Father stopped here many times, staring at something only he could see. I often wondered if he was remembering seeing the woman, Mira throw herself off the cliff. So, before the devil could spit again, he yelled, 'Stop!' Losing sight of the two as the spray covered them. He hung his head, fearing the worst. After a moment, he lifted his eyes to the moon, and there they stood in front of him with moonlight shining all around them. Father always ended his story without telling what had caused the young lovers to seek out Devil's Bridge, but it such a powerful one I'll share it with you.

Maizie and Jeremiah fell in love while working on the neighboring farm. The cruel master refused to let them marry, but he made them share a room with one bed and told them their whelp would belong to him. If it were a girl, she'd join his bed at the age of ten. A boy would be sold to the highest bidder as soon as he could walk. Mortified, the young couple plotted their escape to Devil's Bridge. They comforted each other with the thought the tide would carry their bodies home to Africa—this being the common belief among the slaves.

Father acquired several slaves through the years from other owners. Some he purchased, but when he introduced them as having come from the moon beams, I knew he'd pulled them from the mouth of despair at the Gates of Hell."

"That's some story, Wendy." Cian shivered next to me.

"How did you meet Ethan, Wendy?" I hoped to restore the cheerful mood with the question.

Wendy smiled and opened her mouth, but Ethan interrupted. "Allow me to tell this story." At her nod he continued, "I'd been on the island less than a week, talking with the sugar mill owners about exporting rum. I'd heard rumors of the owner of Wendy Palm's headstrong, crippled daughter, who didn't realize her limitations. I paid no mind to the talk, because I failed to see how it would affect me." He leaned forward, resting his forearms on his thighs and dropped his head, shaking it side to side.

"Go on and skip to the part of how much you love me and couldn't bear to live without me," Wendy said.

Ethan continued shaking his head.

"You might wish to get on with the story before I clobber you."

"You'll not raise a hand to me, woman," Ethan said raising his head. "This is my tale. I'll tell it as I see fit."

His words made all of us chuckle but Wendy rolled her eyes.

"A local told me about a cave with a pool of liquid glass containing tiny creatures that'd cure you of any ails."

It sounded like Glass Water Cave. I squeezed Cian's hand and leaned forward to ensure I heard every word.

"Not that I believed such nonsense, but being a novice spelunker, I wanted to explore the cave and see the pool of liquid glass. So, I set out on my horse, Goliath. Goliath and I were newly acquainted. We didn't fully trust each other right yet. I came to a lookout spot with a magnificent view of the island's coast. Not too surprised to see another horse tied to a tree, since I knew others made it a habit to dip in the pool. I hoofed it on foot from there." He paused, taking a deep breath and shaking his head. "You will never guess who I came upon trying her best to make it down the steep incline of gravel. The sugar plantation's crippled daughter, Wendy! There she stood with her two walking sticks leaning against the cliff face. Her clothes wet with sweat, dust on her cheeks and arms."

His description had me stealing a glance at Wendy to see how she took it. She sat with a stiff back and chin lifted high.

"I said, 'Good afternoon, Miss Kincaid. Forgive me for asking, but is this a walk you should be taking?' She drew herself up tall, puffed put her chest, and Cupid smote me right then."

Out of the corner of my eye, I saw Wendy's frame relax at Ethan's

145

declaration.

"She looked like she'd bathed in a vat of pride, and I'd never seen anyone look so beautiful. I reckoned she wanted to dip in the famed pool for its healing properties, so I offered to help her. When she told me she could make it to the pool on her own, I knew better than to waste time arguing. So, I picked her up and carried her down with her hitting and fussing at me all the way! Such a sight we made, for all the ruckus she kicked up caused me to slip a time or two. By the time I reached the cave, both of us were dusty and grimy. Sitting her on the ground at the mouth of the cave, I climbed down inside, then turned to look up at her. I said, 'Do you prefer to sit there looking pretty, or would you like me to help you down into the water?'"

A faint blush spread across Wendy's face. Smiling, Ethan continued his tale.

"She blushed just like she is now. She let me help her into the water and we spent most of the day there. Taught her how to swim and captured her heart." He lifted her hand to his lips and kissed it, never taking his eyes off hers.

"On the way out of the cave, he pulled a knife out of his boot and carved his initials and mine, declaring his love. He did win my heart that day. He made me feel safe, cared for, and cherished."

"Ye won't believe it, but Irelyn and I saw yer carving in the future. We recognized your initials, Wendy, not thinking they could possibly be yours, due to the length of time past."

"Now we know the story behind the carving. I'm happy for you both." I smiled at the two of them.

The mood grew somber and quiet, so I told them about the future. Enthralled, they asked to hear more and more. My description of Cian's driving only ensued more laughter. Finally, the dying fire called the evening to an end.

CHAPTER 29
Revelations

"**M**s. Calleah, do you have a minute?" I said. Cian and I had sought her out. We found her shelling peas at a wooden table behind the main house, underneath the kitchen windows.

"Don't nobody own time. Only fools think to control it." She looked up from the peas but her hands kept shelling. "I been wondering when you'd come seeking answers."

I stole a glance at Cian. He nodded and we sat down across from her at the weathered table. Sitting in the shade of the house, the breeze cooled my skin. I took a moment to enjoy it, gathering my thoughts. Cian and I had spent our days doing what we could to help clean up after the French soldier's destructive raid on the island. I stretched out my legs and leaned back in the chair with my arms over my head, arching my back.

"Feel better now, do ye, Irelyn?" Amusement shone from Cian's eyes.

"You didn't join me here because you sought cover from the sun. What do you need of me?" She continued shelling the peas.

Clearing my throat, I began. "You helped me return to my own time once. Then, you helped Cian come to my time. Our daughter..." Not sure how to put my question into words, I paused. Cian picked up where I left off.

"When Irelyn and I traveled it was under a Blue Moon, and we had ye to help, besides—"

"Except when I came to the past the first time," I said finding my voice again. "That can be accredited to Granddad Irish's stone and a Blue Moon."

I wasn't sure what to think of the way Ms. Calleah inhaled deeply and let it out.

"Yes, yes." Cian motioned at me. "But our wee lassie, she appears to have traveled to the past and back without a Blue Moon, or ye to help her."

"She did have the stone, though, and there may have been a blue fairy involved." I interjected.

"Ah, the faeries, they guard all things mystical. That would explain her travel to the past."

"When she came back, she brought a boy with her."

Ms. Calleah's hands went still and she looked up at me. "You'd do well to learn about the boy. It could be he's the traveler."

Traveler? I had never considered that scenario, and looking at Cian's furrowed brow it didn't appear he had thought of it either.

"As for your own," Ms. Calleah said standing, "maybe she is, maybe she isn't. Time will tell." She walked up the steps to the kitchen, taking the shelled peas with her but leaving us a little shell shocked. Pausing on the top step, she turned. "Some folks are prone to it. They have wandering souls. Wandering souls will always find the passages." She nodded once and made to go in.

"Wait. Do ye mean to say it's possible to go home any time?" Cian jumped up and began pacing. "Why did ye have me wait 'til a blue moon if not necessary, when I wanted to go forward to find Irelyn?" Cian seemed agitated. I hoped it didn't have anything to do with him feeling more comfortable in his own time.

Ms. Calleah shook her head. "I'll try to explain, again. You belonged here. To go when you no belong, Blue Moon helps. Can't hurt. There be places open to travel. That, you need, but not always work. Blue Moon makes sure it work, along with a good reason or strong desire. See?"

Trying to get it straight in my own mind, I said, "So the Blue Moon is like a back-up or enhancer to the special places. But one also has to have a good reason or be determined, or be a traveler?"

"Yes!" Smiling, she clapped her hands together.

"But, what about now? Cian belongs here. Wouldn't he need a Blue Moon, while I wouldn't?" I avoided his intent gaze on my face, waiting for an answer.

"No. He no longer belongs to this time. This time has no more hold on him. He has love and passion with you, and he has pure love for his daughter. Now, he belongs to your time."

Tears spilled from my eyes, relieved I wouldn't have to leave Cian behind at all. He squeezed my hand.

"How do we—you'll help us, Calleah?" My voice grew thick with emotion.

"Yes, I help. My brother filled my head with lies about the two of you. I see the truth of you and of him too. He grew wicked at a young age. I'm sorry for the things he done."

"Don't worry yourself about it." I rose from my knees and rushed up the stairs to hug her. "All has turned out all right."

"We have some goodbyes to say and some graves to see, then we'll be ready." Cian took my elbow and led me away.

Walking hand in hand, I couldn't help smiling. Ms. Calleah had lifted a great load from me. Not only could we both go home, but we could go whenever we chose. Not to mention, when we got home, Cal would no longer be a threat.

Cian's head turned, giving me a sideways glance. "I'm glad to see the spring in yer step now, but do ye mind telling me what the tears were about earlier?"

Heat rose in my cheeks at the thought of sharing my fear, but he had a right to know. "I grew afraid you'd choose to remain in your own time." At his look of astonishment, I rushed on to explain. "Oh, I know you'd not stay, you're too honorable and loyal for that. But, I feared you'd wish to, and you might come to resent me."

"Look at me." He stopped, turning my body to face him. I couldn't bare to do as he commanded. He placed a finger under my chin and raised it until my eyes met his. My heart skipped a beat at the love and passion shining from his eyes. "Irelyn, I love ye so. I followed ye to the future as soon as I grew old enough and became a free man. I've never regretted it—ever. Even if ye didn't love me, I still would need to be in the same time as ye. Remember the stones we dropped in the Glass Water Cave? In deep, troubled or still waters, we're in it together. Aye?"

"Aye." My lips met his, consumed with a hunger for more. After a few seconds, Cian drew back, holding me at arms-length.

"We best be getting along before I take ye right here."

The thought made me chuckle rather than recoil away.

"I mean it," he said pulling me into a walking gait again. "Look, we're here." A plot of land with four stones lay to our left. "The stones are Mr. and Mrs. Kincaid and Ma and Da. When Ma died..." His voice grew thick. He cleared his throat. "Mr. Kincaid said she and Da had become his family, and he wouldn't hear of either of them being buried anywhere but the Kincaid family plot."

Looking around, I couldn't tell without the usual land markers if we were in the same plot we found Wendy and her family buried. "Is this where Wendy is eventually buried?"

"Yes. I looked for these four graves when I first went to our time."

Hearing him say "our time" filled me with peace.

"There were so many more burial sights, and nothing looked the same. I never did find them. I guess they were destroyed, moved, or no longer legible."

"That's a shame. Let's go see them now." I stopped to pick several fragrant Plumeria flowers to lay on Brian and Ina's graves. In silence, I sat beside him at the graves.

Cian reached forward, resting his hand on the ground where his parents lay. "I love ye, Ma. Miss ye, Da. Ye'd love our wee lassie, so."

"Thank you for giving me Cian." Filled with so much gratitude I didn't know what else to say.

The walk back to the plantation took little time. I wanted to say goodbye to Wendy and Ethan, but Wendy refused to come downstairs.

"I don't like goodbyes," Wendy yelled down to us. "And we've already had one this lifetime."

Ethan looked embarrassed by his wife's behavior, but I understood. She loved us, as we did her. Etan shook Cian's hand and clapped his shoulder, but I reached up and hugged Ethan's neck.

We had only been back in the past for three days, but Cian and I now stood in the same spot I had as a young girl. A place Cian stood years later as a young man.

Chanting, Calleah walked circles around us. Her circling brought to my memory the fairies in the forest spiraling around me as a young girl. A sudden wind whipped and everything began to spin. I clung to Cian's arm. He squeezed my hand.

CHAPTER 30
Resolutions
Present Day, Antiqua

The sun filtering through the tropical leaves above me danced across my face, waking me up. I breathed in the saltwater mixed with the plumeria scent of our cove. Only Heaven could smell better to me. So lighthearted and content, the worry and depression that plagued me since Erin went missing no longer did.

Cian still slept beside me but I thought it best to let him wake on his own. I kicked off my shoes and walked down to the water. Just out of reach of the tide, I rolled up my pant legs, allowing the waves to wash over my feet and rise up to my calves. The receding waves left numerous tiny clam shells to burrow back under the sand.

Turning around to check on Cian, I saw he sat watching me. I smiled and went to join him.

"Don't stop on my account. Ye make a fetching scene."

"Well, Mr. Gallagher, what now?" I plopped down beside him in the sand.

"Ye mean after we make love on our own private beach?" His leering expression made it clear he wasn't joking.

"Mmm, although your suggestion has its merits, I'd prefer to skip the sand. How about we check in with our daughter and figure out how long we've been gone? Then I'll make my move on you in our bedroom with the terrace doors open, so we can hear the waves crashing against the cliff."

"Will ye light the candle that smells so good?" He stood and extended a hand for me.

"Yes, I will."

"Deal. Let's go!"

Inside the bungalows screened in porch, I sat with Rosa. We sipped lemonade while Emilio and Cian installed a winch on my jeep.

Our three day adventure back to the past had only equaled one day in the present. Emilio and Rosa weren't even aware we had been gone.

"When does our girl return?" Rosa fanned herself with a small woven-palm-leaf fan Erin gave her for Easter.

"She gets home the day after tomorrow. Do you think they need some help?" I inclined my head to the guys who looked to be having trouble with the winch.

"Nah, they'll figure it out." Sitting forward in her chair, she called out to the men. "Hey, fellas, I made you some strawberry lemonade and the empanadas are about ready to come out of the oven." She returned to her resting position, giving her drink a sip. "That'll give them incentive. So, how are the two of you going to spend your last full day together?"

"We're going to ride bikes over to the cemetery and look around. Many of the tombstones are ancient."

Her head shake showed me how unexciting she thought that idea was, but she raised her glass. "To each their own."

The oven timer went off, signaling time to set the table. I laid out plates, napkins, and silverware. Rosa retrieved the garden salad from the fridge. The men walked in before either of us had a chance to call them.

After washing up, the four of us sat around the kitchen table eating Rosa's meat empanadas and the garden salad I chopped and mixed. Her empanadas never disappointed—I'd never eaten better ones.

Scooting back from the table, Cian patted his stomach. "Irelyn, what do ye say to a bike ride to the cemetery now to work off this food?"

Our ride to the cemetery ended up being more of a race than an easy-going pedal. I was too anxious to see if the dates of Wendy's death and her baby boy's read differently since our little jaunt to the past. Cian hadn't said anything about the pace of our ride, so he probably felt the same.

The bikes we left against the gate and entered the yard, walking to the same area where we found Wendy's grave the first time. Before, nothing set the Kincaid and Whitaker stones apart from the rest of the stones in the cemetery. Now, there stood an elaborate, scrolled iron gate with an iron fence surrounding the tombs.

I gasped and entered ahead of Cian. "Look, Wendy and Ethan have a joint stone. Come read what it says."

"Lived to a ripe old age," Cian read the words aloud, "beholden to dear friends."

"And here's their baby boy, Christopher. He lived to be seventy-five years old. We saved them, Cian. You saved them."

"Irelyn," he whispered. I knew before even looking, he'd found his parent's markers. They looked almost just as they had back then. "How did…I never mentioned not being able to find Ma and Da's graves to either of them. Did ye?"

"Yes, I told Ethan why it meant so much to us to visit their graves while we were there. It never occurred to me he would or could do something about it."

"It's wonderful. They sectioned off the Kincaid/Whitaker plot, and they've been cared for over the years. Irelyn, we can bring Erin here to honor her ancestors." He swiped a hand across his eyes and I loved him all the more.

"No offense," Sonja said, exhaustion oozing from her tone. "You know we love spending time with your daughter, but, I think we'll wait awhile before having children." She sank into the living room chair, leaving Jorge to take Erin's baggage upstairs.

Chuckling, I raised my hand. "No offense taken. I know exactly what you mean. How did it go with the school?"

"Problem solved. All's well 'til the next crisis. Let's get together for lunch or coffee in a day or two and I'll tell you all about it. I've got to get home and unpack." She stood and caught up to Jorge on his way down the stairs to walk to the door.

"Thank you so much, Sonja. And thanks for dropping her off."

Even her offered wave looked exhausted as she walked out to the porch.

With dinner cooling on the stove top, I had Erin help me set the table. The fresh fish Cian caught and fileted this morning smelled delicious—pan fried in cornmeal then roasted with okra in the oven. Adding corn on the cob insured Erin would eat at least one vegetable.

"Where be me world traveler?" Cian came in from the barn acting like he didn't see Erin.

"Here I am, Da!" She jumped up for him to lift her above his head. Her squeals ended at the chair Cian sat her in for dinner.

"Well, Lassie, did ye turn Virginia on its head?"

Giggling, Erin said, "No, Da, but we ate the best pizza in the whole world, and Auntie Sonja showed me where Mommy lived when she was my age. Oh! I got to spend a whole day in school with the big kids, first grade!"

"Did ye now? I'm glad ye had fun. Now, bow yer head so we can say a blessing for our food."

Her little head gave a dutiful bow and she clasped her hands in front of her. Cian winked at me, taking hold of my hand to say the blessing. I felt blessed, indeed, as I bowed my own head.

The next morning, wearing my large, floppy, straw hat, I sat on my knees in the garden, pulling grass and weeds from the poblano peppers. How wonderful to be home, back in the garden with Erin in the coral with her pony, Iris, and Cian. Working in the garden quieted me, filling me with tranquility.

Introduced to the poblano pepper by Rosa, I fell in love. A pepper full of flavor without being spicy, or picoso as Rosa would say. They grew so plentiful I looked for recipes to add them to—one of my favorites being omelets with mozzarella cheese, a little cream cheese and poblano peppers. Hmm...omelets for lunch didn't sound like a bad idea.

Lost in my lunch plans, my cell phone going off to the tune of What A Wonderful World, startled me. I stood up, pulling off the garden gloves to pull my phone out of the pocket in my shorts.

"Hello, Irelyn here." I walked to the porch to sit in the shade.

"Irelyn? It's your cousin Jewell. How are you, dear?"

"Hi, Jewell. I'm doing great. We all are. How's Ian doing? Has he started his schooling yet?"

"Actually, that's why I called. He's a bright boy, but he doesn't like his studies and there's so much he doesn't know. We're easily annoyed with each other. I thought a little trip might be just the thing. We can make it part of our Geography lesson, as well as our Science lesson by studying the insects and plants native to the islands and surrounding waters. What do you think? I've been looking at a hotel but wanted to make sure the timing is right with the three of you. We've been a mite lonely since you left. Colleen doesn't get to come around much, it being their busy season. Every season is their busy season. Well?"

"Oh, Jewell, we'd absolutely love it! Don't even think of booking a hotel. Erin will be so pleased. Cian too, of course. How soon can you come?"

"How about next week? That will give us time to pack and ask old Mr. Patrick to watch the sheep."

"Perfect! I'm so excited, Jewell."

"I'll call to let you know our flight date and time. I'm going to go tell Ian the good news. He'll be so excited. Good talking to you." She clicked off the phone.

I bounded down the steps and sprinted to the corral. "Cian! Erin! Guess who's coming to visit?" Out of breath, I leaned against the corral rail. Clearly, I needed to do that more often.

"Who's coming to visit us?" Cian joined me at the rail and leaned across for a kiss.

"Is it Liam and his momma, Cora?" Erin continued around the corral on the back of Iris.

Liam and Cora lived in a whole different time. I couldn't imagine she would ever see them again. I looked to Cian for input but he shrugged his shoulders.

"No, it's cousin Jewell and Ian! They're coming all the way from Ireland. Neither of them have ever been to the Caribbean. We'll be sure to make their vacation extra special."

"Yea! When, Mommy? When? Tomorrow?"

"They'll be here next week. So, we have time to plan their visit." On Iris's next pass by, I reached out and gave her a pat.

"Glad I'll be to see them without having to step on a plane." Cian grinned at me.

"I thought you might feel that way." I patted his handsome face before going back to the porch to call Rosa.

"Buenas tardes, Irelyn."

Her cheerful greeting brought a smile to my lips. "Hi, Rosa. Jewell and her newly adopted, eight-year-old son, Ian, are coming for a visit next week. Do you think you could help out with the food while they're here?" I bit my lip, waiting for her answer.

"Isn't that wonderful? I'd be glad to. Erin hasn't stopped talking about him. Maybe I can get Jewell to share some of her Irish recipes with me."

"I'm sure you can get at least one out of her. You'll love her, Rosa. She's real friendly, just like you. Thanks a lot. Love you!"

"De nada. Love you too. Adios!"

I slipped the phone back into my pocket to raise my arms above my head. I clasped my hands and bent side to side for a good stretch. No time like the present to finish clearing the grass and weeds from the garden. Everything needed to look perfect for next week's visit. Maybe I'd even give the garden gate a fresh coat of white paint—that would spiff it up.

Putting my gloves back on, I walked over to the garden, humming. At the gate I looked to see if it could use a fresh coat.

Arms wrapped around me from behind, lifting me into the air.

"I know what ye be thinking, Irelyn," Cian said setting me back down. "Ye don't need to go overboard. They'll love us all the same."

"Hmm. When did you and Emilio paint the barn last?" I had to bite the inside of my cheek to keep from smiling.

"Sheesh. I'd better go warn Emilio to stay clear of ye."

"Don't go too far, it's lunch time. I'm thinking of making omelets."

"Sounds great. If I dice up the potatoes, will ye skillet fry them to eat with the omelets? Erin is brushing down Iris right now. I told her to come see you when she's done, incase ye need her help."

"Deal. Thanks. She can work on the garden while I make lunch."

Between the three of us, one week would be plenty of time to spiff the place up before Jewell and Ian arrived.

CHAPTER 31
A Life Full and Complete

The plumeria lei I held in my hands smelled fantastic. I'd strung enough together using flowers Cian gathered from Shell Cove to make three. One for each of us to hold. The three of us stood at the airport baggage claim waiting for Jewell and Ian.

"Erin! Over here!"

The yelling, which sounded like Ian, came from behind me. I turned and spotted him jumping up and down, waving his arms. Jewell came up behind him wheeling a carry on beside her, appearing a mite bedraggled.

Cian placed his lei on Ian and Erin and I adorned Jewell with ours.

Holding her leis to her face, she inhaled. "Just the pick me up I needed. A heavenly scent to be sure."

"Glad ye like them. They're all over our property." Cian grabbed their two suitcases off the turnstile.

"I can't hardly wait for you to see Shell Cove. The Plumerias and Hibiscus are all in bloom right now." I led the way to the Jeep, making sure Ian and Erin each held a hand.

"Erin can wear my lei. Girls like flowers more than boys. We don't wear flowers." He handed the lei to Erin, who gladly slipped it over her head.

Judging by Jewell's frequent exclamations on the ride to the house, the island enchanted her. Sonja and Jorge met us on the porch, standing between two large Boston Ferns. They waved as we pulled up. The moment the tires stopped rolling Erin and Ian jumped out of the Jeep.

"Come on, Ian! Let's say hi to my pony, Iris!"

Smiling, I called out after them. "I'll bring lunch out to you for a picnic in the barn." With all the company inside, there wouldn't be enough seats in the house.

After Cian's quick introductions, we all turned to enter the house. Sonja looped her arm through mine.

"Rosa out did herself. I believe I need to come over more often—on second thought—I'd better stay away." She patted her hips.

Jorge, always close by, grabbed Sonja by the hips. "I like a little meat on the hips. Gives me something to hold onto."

Sonja swatted at his hands, laughing. "Behave yourself or you'll be sent out to the barn with the kids." She looked over her shoulder. "Sorry, Jewell. We really do know how to act in polite company."

"Oh, goodness be. Don't mind me, you make me feel right at home. Reminds me of gathering with my aunt and uncles and their spouses. A lively bunch they were."

Inside the kitchen lunch had been laid out. Chicken and sour cream enchiladas—my personal favorite—also Spanish rice and guacamole with chips. Rosa had gone all out and even made sopapillas.

"What you do, see, is bite off one of the corners." Heat rose from the sopapilla Emilio held in one hand. "Then, you pour honey into it."

Jewell nodded, paying rapt attention to Emilio's demonstration.

"That's the proper way to eat a sopapilla." He dusted cinnamon sugar off his fingertips.

"I think I must try it for myself." Jewell licked her lips.

The moment I noticed Jewell's eyes getting droopy I concluded our little welcome luncheon. Even though the airplane landed in the morning, to Jewell and Ian, it felt like three pm—Antigua being four hours earlier than Cork. An eight hour flight would wear anyone out.

Sonja and Jorge helped Rosa and Emilio clean up from lunch. Cian walked out to the barn to check on the 'wee ones' as he liked to call Ian and Erin. I led Jewell to the stairs.

"Oh, wait. What about Ian and the luggage?"

I patted her arm. "Don't worry, Cian is headed to the barn as we speak, and he'll bring the luggage up afterwards." We climbed the stairs to the second level. "I put you in the room next to Erin. There's a bathroom between you. Ian's room is across from yours. Cian and I are the level above. I'll show you around after you rest."

"Sounds lovely."

"Lay down and have a nice nap. Rest up, we have a lot planned for you."

"Don't mind if I do. Please thank Rosa for a lovely lunch." She lay down on the queen-sized sleigh bed. I closed the door and went back down to the kitchen.

My four friends had the cleanup well taken care of. I decided to join Cian and the kids. I came across Cian stacking firewood in the fire pit. Along came Erin and Ian toting more wood.

"I take it we're having a bonfire tonight?"

"Nah, nothing as big as a bonfire, mind ye, just a cozy fire to sit by while ye gaze at the stars."

"And roast marshmallows!" Ian grinned.

"Mommy, can we make smores?"

"I think that could be arranged."

"What's a smore?" Ian said.

"It's yummy, that's what!" Erin dropped her small bundle next to the circle.

The idea of a fire with smores, helped Sonja, Jorge, Rosa and Emilio decide to stick around for an evening under the stars. So, we set the lawn chairs out and made an afternoon of it, enjoying each other's company and watching the kids ride Iris.

About two hours later Jewell joined us looking refreshed. The girls and I walked her around the property, showing her the garden, fruit trees, barn, chickens, and the cliff.

"Oh, Irelyn, it's absolutely breathtaking." She held a hand over her chest.

"Later, I'll show you the view from our balcony. The view is spectacular from up there."

"The palm trees are so stately. Stunning." She shaded her eyes, gazing up at the palms.

"They're Royal Palms. They've been here since the 1600's, when this property was part of a sugar plantation."

"My goodness, such history. That makes them about four hundred years old!"

"Royal Palms can live seven hundred years. Can you imagine?" I loved the idea of looking upon the same trees as Wendy had—a lasting connection between us. I led Jewell on, excited to show her more.

"Is there a sugar mill still on the property?"

"Unfortunately, it didn't survive. There is one from that era on the island, though. We can see it while out sightseeing."

"Great! I hope Ian hasn't been any trouble for you today while I napped."

"Not at all. He and Erin helped Cian with the fire wood. Since then, they've been riding Iris."

"Well, glad to hear it. I hope this trip does him good. He needed the break. I needed the break." She gave me a half smile.

"Tomorrow, he'll enjoy Shell Cove. We'll take a picnic and swim."

"Ma! Look at me! See what I can do?" Ian sat atop Cian's russet colored horse, Aubry, waving one arm at us.

Ma? I looked at Jewell with my eyebrows raised in question.

"Yes, he calls me Ma now." She wiped moisture from her eyes and laughed. "Forgive me, I'm emotional."

"Well, of course you are. That's wonderful, Jewell." I gave her a brief hug then continued our walk toward the barnyard.

Ian guided Aubry around the yard like he'd been born on the back of a horse. "Watch! I can make her walk backward." Ian leaned back in the saddle and gently used his legs to apply pressure toward the back of the horse. Astonishing enough, Aubry stepped backward until Ian sat straight in the saddle.

My mouth fell open. I looked to the men. "Who taught him how to do that?"

"That's just the thing, no one. The lad's a natural horseman."

"I'm so proud of you, Ian. You're amazing!" Jewell pulled her phone out and took his picture. Puffing his chest out, he beamed almost as bright as the sun. "I guess I'm going to have to get that boy a horse. It will be a help with the sheep, for sure." Jewell's face beamed with pride.

"Da, let me try. I can do it too," Erin said, her tone full of demand.

Before Cian could open his mouth to reply, Ian did. "You're barely older than a toddler. Stick to your purple pony."

Erin clenched her fists at her side, stomped her foot, and put her fists on her hips. "Her name is Iris, and she's not purple! I am five and a half years old, and I can do anything you can do. Probably better, cuz you're just a stupid boy!"

Jewell's hand covered her mouth. It didn't appear she knew how to defuse the situation. Cian, looked to be trying his best not to laugh. No help there. It came down to me.

"Erin, Why don't you show Jewell and Ian the trick uncle Jorge taught you? I bet Ian has never seen it." Her eyes lit up and off she ran to get Iris. Jewell spoke quietly to Ian, and he swung a leg over the saddle and slid off Aubry.

The moment we all had a seat, Jorge made an announcement. "Ladies and gentlemen, please allow me to introduce to you all, the extraordinary Miss Erin and her delightful pony, Iris." He stepped aside and Erin came around the corner standing on top of her saddle, holding Iris's reins.

I'd seen her do this a hundred times, but I held my breath nonetheless. Everyone cheered, including Ian. I wondered what Jewell had said to him. After making a round, Erin jumped into Jorge's arms.

"Now that all the horse demonstrations are over, I deem it time for smores." I raised my voice for everyone to hear. The sun had dropped low on the horizon, signaling time to light the fire.

Cian brought his guitar out while Emilio lit the fire. We pulled our chairs in a circle around the burning logs. Cian handed the guitar to Jorge. "Play something for us."

Accompanied by music, Rosa and I got the items for smores. Erin stopped dancing around the fire long enough to roast her marshmallow and assemble a smore. Everyone enjoyed their sticky, gooey treat. Even Jorge set down the guitar long enough to make a smore and eat it in two big bites.

"It's the best thing I've ever eaten," Ian said with little bits of gooey marshmallow stuck to the corners of his mouth.

The men sat around the fire, staying until it died out. Jewell and I, accompanied by Rosa and Sonja, took the kids in to bathe and put them to bed. Rosa and Sonja got a bottle of wine and glasses from the kitchen.

"We'll save you a glass," Sonja said going into the living room to make themselves comfortable.

I smiled and continued up the stairs with Jewell, Ian, and Erin. After spending the day surrounded by our friends, my life felt full and complete.

CHAPTER 32
Second Wishes

"Faster, Da, faster!" Erin squealed in the backseat of the Jeep, along with me and Ian. Jewel sat in the front seat, wearing a scarf I loaned her to protect her hair from the wind. Her hands gripped the handle in front of her in a white-knuckled hole.

Cian had taken the top and doors off the Jeep. He drove us around the property at accelerated speeds, bumping us off our seats, drawing cheers and shouts from the kids.

He drove up to the paved road and stopped to check for traffic. I released a pent-up breath I didn't even realize I held. On the main road we followed the coast of the island, with its spectacular views of the cerulean blue waters.

At a roadside stand selling tropical drinks in a coconut, Cian pulled over. The five of us sat at a picnic table shaded by a banana tree, sipping our delicious concoctions.

"The island is lovely, for sure. I can see why you stay instead of coming home to live in Cork. Not a sheep to be seen anywhere on the island."

"Every once in a while we talk about moving to Ireland, but it always comes down to our friends being here. They've become our family too. It'd be hard to leave them, especially since Sonja followed me here from Virginia. I don't think she'd take too kindly to me leaving now."

"Maybe one day when our wee Erin is ready to go off to college." Cian and I smiled at each other at the thought.

"What else are we gonna see?" Ian bounced on the bench.

Erin bounced right along with him. "Yeah, Da, let's go!"

"All right, load up into the Jeep and we'll be off with the wind." Cian took the scenic route back to the house, but really, all routes were scenic on the island. Even when the coastal waters couldn't be seen, the hibiscus, plumeria and other flowering trees and bushes made any drive on the island worth seeing.

The Jeep rolled to a stop in front of the house, and the kids were not lax in hopping out. I called out to their backs as they ran up the steps to the porch, "Get your swim suits on, we're going to the cove!"

Inside the kitchen, I couldn't help but notice the cooler sitting on the floor and the picnic basket on top of it. Attached to the basket was a note from Rosa.

> I took the liberty of packing lunch.
> Please enjoy! Emilio and I may join you later.
>
> Love, Rosa

At Cian's entrance I laid the note on the counter. "What would I do without her?"

His strong arms wrapped around me, and said over my head, "I suspect ye'd get by just fine. I might be a bit skinnier, though."

I jabbed him in the gut, not too hard though—he kind of spoke the truth.

Ahead of all of us on the path to the cove, Ian and Erin skipped. By the time I reached the cove, Ian lay in the hammock. Erin stood close by, giving him instructions on how to properly get in and out of it—our little miss know it all.

"I'm in it aren't I? I don't need some little girl telling me how to do anything." He spoke with such disdain.

"Fine!" Erin gave him a push and stomped off to the beach.

The shift of movement made Ian lose his weight distribution. The hammock turned him out, face down in the sand. In seconds, he jumped to his feet and took off after Erin.

At seeing him coming, she ran and dove into the surf, looking like a young dolphin. Cian had taught her well. However, when Ian did the same, my mouth fell open.

Jewel shrugged. "He's just a natural...at everything, it would appear."

Catching up to Erin in the water, he dunked her under——splashing and laughter ensued. I relaxed, seeing no evidence of lasting hard feelings between the two. Jewel, Cian, and I settled into chairs with a cold drink.

The three of us sat there sipping our drinks and munching on the fruit and cheese Rosa packed until the kids ran up, sprinkling us with salty water.

"Look, Ma! It's an octopus! A real live octopus!" Ian held a small octopus in one hand, its head no bigger than a quarter with long tentacles hanging down through his fingers.

"She's purple!" Erin's exclamation made Ian scowled at her.

"Oh my, would you look at that tiny creature. He is purple! I've never seen an octopus."

"I've never seen one so small or purple. Maybe ye should put it back in the water, lad."

"Yes, we don't want to hurt it," I said.

Ian and Erin walked back until they stood in a foot of water. I followed, along with the other adults, to watch the small purple creature in its natural element. Ian bent over and let the water wash it off his hand. The octopus floated to the sandy bottom and moved across the ocean floor using his long tentacles to reach deeper water. I stood silent, amazed at what I'd just witnessed.

"Let's eat, shall we?" Cian clapped his hands together.

The kids ran to the chairs and spread out the sheet we brought. I followed more slowly, staying with Cian and Jewell.

"This cove is truly an amazing place," Jewell said.

"Yes, I don't know how we'd ever leave it." I reached for Cian's hand.

Unpacking the rest of Rosa's food, I found fried chicken, veggie sticks, chips, and oatmeal raisin cookies—Cian's favorite. In the basket I found plates and napkins.

Feeling full, I stayed in my chair, insisting the kids stay out of the water for a while. They needed to give their food time to digest as much as I did. They took turns burying each other in the sand, happy to stay out of the water for a bit.

"Ye know, Irelyn, we wouldn't have to sell the bungalow or Shell Cove. We could sell our house and move to Ireland. Then we could spend our anniversary at Shell Cove every year."

"Something to consider." I frowned thinking of leaving our friends. I noticed Ian kept rubbing his arms, body, and head. "Ian, are you okay? Is the sand itching you?"

"No, Ma'am. My skin feels like it's vibrating the closer I am to the big rock over there."

My gaze snapped to Jewel to gage her reaction, but she had drifted to sleep and didn't appear to hear him. But Cian stared at the boy with wide eyes. Yes, he would understand all too well what Ian might be feeling, but we didn't need to alarm the boy.

"Well, let's make sure to stay far from the rock. Okay?"

"Sure." Ian nodded. "I don't like how it feels."

"I think ye stayed out of the water long enough, if ye want to go in for a swim with me."

"Yeah!" Both children cheered. Shaking off the sand, they raced to the water with Cian on their heels.

Joined by Rosa and Emilio we ended up staying until the first star appeared in the sky. On our return to the house, Jewell accompanied Ian upstairs to see he got a bath and she planned to shower herself. Cian, too, went up to shower. Erin ran to the barn to tell Iris good night. I followed her but not with as much energy.

Her soft chatter, loud enough to carry outside the barn door, made me stop. I loved listening to the things she shared with Iris. She's always spoke to the animal like she could understand her.

"See, granny Oleta? The Druid King will grant my wishes. He's already granted one, and one day I'll have my own prince charming like Mommy and Da."

Chills raced across my arms and down my spine, weakening my knees. Granny Oleta? Like Mommy and Da? The words echoed through my mind.

Wish Upon A Blue Moon is Danna Walters' second novel in her Blue Moon YA series. She remains intrigued by Ireland and it's folklore. Her great grandfather was Irish, so Danna feels her love for the Emerald Isle comes naturally to her.